"There's something I have to tell you."

Lynsey's voice was muffled as her cheek pressed against Madoc's chest.

"That you love me, eh?" He was so indulgent, his voice so warm, that she wanted to do anything but tell him the truth.

"It's true that I do," she answered, "but it's not that this time. I...it's...I'm not expecting a child after all."

She felt him go rigid. He pushed her arms away. There was a space between them now, a few paces that might have been a million miles.

"So I was tricked into this marrigage," Madoc snarled, turning away from her.

Lynsey winced at the bitterness, the acrimony in his tone. How could she say "It's true that I love you"? He would never believe that now.

LILIAN PEAKE lives near the sea in England. Her first job was working for a mystery writer, employment that she says gave her an excellent insight into how an author functions. She went on to become a journalist and reported on the fashion world for a trade magazine. Later she took on an advice column, the writing of which contributed to her understanding of people's lives. Now she draws on her experiences and perception, not to mention a fertile imagination, to craft her many fine romances. She and her husband, a college principal, have three children.

Books by Lilian Peake

HARLEQUIN PRESENTS
454—STRANGERS INTO LOVERS
474—ACROSS A CROWDED ROOM
496—DAY OF POSSESSION
524—BITTER REVENGE
612—PASSIONATE INTRUDER
886—ICE INTO FIRE

HARLEQUIN ROMANCE
2220—REBEL IN LOVE
2279—STRANGER ON THE BEACH
2404—PROMISE AT MIDNIGHT
2603—NIGHT OF POSSESSION
2614—COME LOVE ME
2651—A WOMAN IN LOVE

These books may be available at your local bookseller.

LILIAN PEAKE

elusive paradise

Harlequin Books

TORONTO • NEW YORK • LONDON
AMSTERDAM • PARIS • SYDNEY • HAMBURG
STOCKHOLM • ATHENS • TOKYO • MILAN

For my friend
Margaret Matthews
of Abilene, Texas

Harlequin Presents first edition January 1987
ISBN 0-373-10949-0

Original hardcover edition published in 1985
by Mills & Boon Limited

CHAPTER ONE

THE young man leaned forward and placed his half-empty glass on the table.

'So tell us, Lynsey,' he coaxed, 'what you think is going to happen.'

His friends and companions seated around the table were dressed in their best, some wearing white carnations. They were all of them more serious than guests usually are at a wedding reception.

The cake had been cut and distributed, the champagne toasts had been drunk, the bridal couple were mingling. A small, colourful group provided the music and the tables had been cleared for dancing.

Lynsey shook her head at the question and pushed at her deep brown hair. 'I don't know, Des, and I doubt if Lantern Scientific management knows, either.'

'All the same,' someone else offered, 'I think there's no doubt about it—the old order changeth, as the saying goes. We can't any of us foresee what's to come.'

'No one knows,' said David, 'who'll stay or go.'

Lynsey agreed with her brother. 'I've heard a rumour that the chairman of Techno-Global is quite ruthless in his business dealings.'

'Which presumably,' Des put in, 'is why the company he's head of rates internationally as one of the giant corporations.'

Lynsey nodded. 'They say he's the man who's made it that way. Rumour also says he's quite heartless in clearing out slack.'

'I heard,' Des remarked, 'about a woman secretary in Techno-Global whose boss got another job. They sacked the secretary without offering her any other position in the company. Worst thing about it was— she had an invalid husband.'

Lynsey frowned in sympathy with the unknown woman. 'A friend of David's used to work for Techno-Global—didn't he, David? He had a wife and three children.'

'Surely he didn't get the push?' asked Carole, a slim young woman with fair hair who held David's hand.

'He did. Ask David. The man at the top took it into his head to give instructions for a head-count, plus an assessment of work.'

Her brother nodded. 'I lost touch with him—he moved to Scotland and he's never contacted me since.'

'You'd better watch out, Lynsey,' Carole said with a rueful smile, 'that the new broom doesn't sweep out your job along with the rubbish.'

Lynsey made a face. 'Not only mine. Research is usually the first thing to suffer and that would affect all of us round this table.'

Her companions groaned at her prophecy.

'And if he's the inhuman robot we're led to believe,' she enlarged, 'he'll probably personally evaluate the job of every single member of Lantern's staff. Now,' she glanced round at the serious faces, 'a wedding's supposed to be a happy occasion, so let's dispel the gloom. Des,' Lynsey flashed a smile at the young man opposite her, 'do you want to dance?'

'Why not?' he answered.

'Then,' she looked around her, 'catch me.' She ran out of the crowded ballroom, seeking somewhere to run. She saw the stairs and made for them across the hotel's entrance foyer.

Carole, his fiancée, turned away with a smile, disappearing into the slow-moving crowd in the softly lighted room.

The man two stairs below had been watching her changing expressions. She coloured at the shrewdness, the minute analysis of his gaze. They were alone on an island of rhythmic sound, a private island undiscovered except by the two of them.

Joking voices reached her, laughter ebbed and flowed, but nothing everyday touched her at that moment. It was as if she was on the brink of discovering some kind of elusive paradise . . .

'Are you ready to go?' His voice, deep and resonant, was part of the very special heaven in which she was wandering.

'Go? Where should I go?' Her voice sounded light, ethereal. He laughed at her bewilderment and her heart somersaulted.

'I found your shoe. It's my reward, you said, to take you home.'

'I didn't mean it,' she declared, confused by the man's electric effect on her. 'I forgot for the moment that my home is over two hundred miles from here. I booked in to this hotel overnight. A lot of us did, for Morwenna's wedding. She's my friend. I work with her, like the others. She invited a lot of us, all from Lantern Scientific.'

The thoughtful eyes considered her. 'I'll take you to your room, instead.'

'No.' Her head shook vigorously. But she had wanted to say 'yes'! This feeling inside me, she panicked, what can I do about it? I don't want to let him out of my sight. I don't want this party to end because then everyone will disperse, including me, and I've got this ridiculous feeling of wanting to follow this man to the ends of the earth. I wish he could take me home, all the way—all those hours together . . . *Yet I don't even know his name.*

In the ballroom, the wedding guests danced, chattered and variously communicated. Lynsey did not feel that she belonged to that crowd any more. She belonged only in that very private world she was sharing with that warm-eyed stranger, a world with a population of two.

Des Parsons appeared in the arched entrance to the ballroom. He frowned and moved his head. 'What about my dance?' he mouthed. But Lynsey looked at him as if she didn't know him. It was as if someone had thrown a net over her, entangling her will-power.

Des looked sourly at her companion and returned to the reception. The man had watched the silent interchange with a studied interest. When Des had gone, he asked softly,

'Will you tell me your name?'

'Lynsey Thorpe.' It had not occurred to her to ask herself, Why should I tell a perfect stranger?

'Lynsey, will you dance?' The request was quietly spoken, his eyes speaking the louder.

She looked at his upturned palm as it moved towards her. The music had become lilting, softly persuasive. She moved down the stairs and stood beside him, resting her hand tentatively in his.

The bride, radiant with the groom at her side, appeared in the doorway of the ballroom. She had changed from her wedding gown and the couple were ready to leave. Guests had gathered around them. Morwenna's eyes flashed round the entrance hall, coming to rest on Lynsey.

She lifted her hand, calling ' 'Bye. I'll be in touch.' Then she caught sight of the man holding her friend's hand. A message sprang into the bride's eyes, urgent and just a little anxious. She shook her head. 'Not him,' she called, 'keep away from him.'

Lynsey's eyes opened wider, then she shook her head, failing to comprehend why Morwenna should be warning her off the man. She must know him, Lynsey reasoned, then she looked up, meeting the quizzical eyes and feeling her heart leap.

Whatever the reason for Morwenna's warning, it had come too late. It would have to be a terrible crime indeed, Lynsey told herself, that would make her want to keep away from this man.

'Madoc,' Morwenna was saying and looking at the man from whom she had urged her friend to keep her distance, 'glad you made it, after all. There's a bit of cake put aside for you. Haven't you got a kiss for the bride?' Morwenna smiled impudently and the man called Madoc dropped Lynsey's hand and pushed through to the bride's side.

The crowd surged towards the couple, taking the stranger with them. Lynsey watched him go, trying to right her world which had been tipped sideways, thinking, this is the end of a story that had no beginning.

The bridal couple were at the door and Lynsey moved forward slowly and sadly. Clouds had drifted across her particular sky, eclipsing that beautiful but fleeting glimpse of heaven. Confetti was being thrown amid shrieks and laughter; it floated everywhere, looking like tinted snow. Lynsey glanced down at herself, brushing her shoulders.

''Bye, Lynsey.' It was Morwenna again, coming up for air from her mother's tearful embrace. ''Bye, Madoc.' The man to whom she had spoken bent down and murmured something and Morwenna went on tiptoe to whisper in his ear. Then she shook her head and gave the man a playful thump on the shoulder.

Everybody followed the couple outside. Lynsey experienced that dive of spirits that occurs when the bride and groom have gone on their way. At least, that was what she told herself as she turned away and went listlessly towards the almost empty ballroom.

So his name was Madoc and Morwenna knew him well. A cousin, maybe, or a friend of her new husband, Griffith? A young girl, one of the bridesmaids, danced up to Lynsey, her pink dress almost to her ankles, a band of tiny flowers around her hair. 'Madoc's my uncle. It's his turn next,' the child announced. 'My mummy says so.'

'Really?' Lynsey's smile was taut. 'Who's the lucky lady?'

'Oh, he's got lots of girlfriends. But Morwenna's his sister, and she's married now, so he's the next, isn't he?' She danced away.

'So now you know,' the deep voice said behind Lynsey, 'why the bride warned you off me.'

Lynsey turned, her heart running up a flight of floating stairs towards the heaven she had so recently glimpsed. No crime, no legal lady in his life, only a joking remark pretending to warn.

'Sisterly rudeness,' she commented, laughing up at him.

His surname, she thought, was Morgan as Morwenna's pre-marital name had been. Madoc Morgan . . . The name had a ring about it, sounded bells inside her head. What kind of bells? *Keep away from him*, Morwenna had urged. I could, Lynsey thought, as much keep away from this man as a bee from a flower, a wave from the shore. We're interlinked, I feel it. The way he's looking at me, does he feel it, too?

'I'm still waiting,' he said, 'for that dance.'

His arm across her shoulders urged her towards the crowd. The dancing had started again, the lull after the couple's departure was over. Lynsey found herself being eased round and against him.

Together they moved slowly, sinuously. The evocative melodies, songs without the words, insinuated themselves into her deepest consciousness. His hold changed, his hands linking behind her, and she found her arms moving upwards of their own volition to cross behind his neck. What was happening to her? she wondered mistily. She had never behaved in this way before.

They danced, waited, maintaining contact, for the music to resume, then danced again. Occasionally, they broke off and Madoc pulled her across to the buffet tables. They ate, standing close, eyes meeting, smiles merging, then danced again. Each time Lynsey returned to his arms, it was like coming in from the cold.

They smiled into each other's eyes and time went by—Lynsey supposed it did—until the evening darkened beyond the windows and the lights came on outside.

She didn't want the day to end. She guessed that people left, since the crowd grew smaller. As if from a distance, she heard her name called now and then, and someone said 'goodbye'. She supposed, also, that she answered.

'Enjoying yourself?' Madoc asked.

'Wonderful.' Her answer was breathless and she didn't care if it told him just how happy he was making her. He indicated the buffet table, which seemed miraculously to have been replenished, but she shook her head.

'It's the best wedding I've ever attended,' she told him, 'certainly the most lavish. Morwenna never told me her parents were rich enough to be able to afford this.'

'She's my parents' only daughter,' he remarked with a wry smile. 'Their son won't cost them a penny. The bride's parents pay,' he reminded her, still smiling, and Lynsey did not waste her time wondering why she found it impossible to smile back.

The thought of this man walking out of her life complete with a beautiful, elegant and wealthy wife on his arm was like walking unclothed into a snowstorm. A shiver went through her and she opened her eyes gladly to the colour and warmth around her.

'You looked so serious,' Madoc teased. 'What's worrying you?'

'Nothing really,' she answered, 'except that I caught a glimpse of the future.'

'And it made you shiver?' His arms tightened as the music drifted on.

His mouth feathered her cheek and she knew she should have protested. Instead, she turned up her face and smiled and his lips whispered across hers. Her pulses were hammering, her whole body was alive. His thighs made contact with hers, so close were they dancing, but not a whisper of her mind's dissent got through to her lips.

She was on a cloud flying towards the sun. If, like Icarus, she flew too near, then she knew the score. Her eyes were drawn to those of the man in whose arms she was moving. She found there a question she had been asked before. Always, in the past, she had said 'no'. How, she questioned herself, am I going to answer this time? His arms closed around her waist and she let her body do the talking.

'Drink?'

Lynsey opened her eyes, surfacing from the music which had paused. Then she nodded, smiling up at him. I'm drunk already, she thought dreamily as he guided her through the chattering couples standing around, so what difference will another drink make?

She thought he had intended going to the bar set up in the ballroom, but he pulled her towards the exit.

Des caught her arm. 'Stay here, Lynsey,' he urged, staring belligerently at her companion. Lynsey looked at him like someone with amnesia. There was, she reflected, only room for two on that cloud she was occupying. Freeing her arm, she moved dreamily in the footsteps of the man who led the way.

The bar was a modern addition, all chrome, black plastic and glass. Scattered around were regular hotel guests. They watched with some curiosity as the couple who had entered, with the glow of someone else's wedding about them, stood waiting to be served.

'What will you have?' Madoc Morgan asked and Lynsey told him. He paid for the drinks, waving away Lynsey's offer to buy her own.

The chairs they chose were pulled together, close to the tall, wide windows. Trees, intensely green, bordered the brown-gravelled drive, while small flowering plants nestled between.

Lynsey looked lingeringly at the scene. Out there was calmness and tranquillity, whereas beside her was a man who had proved himself capable of creating a storm in her life. If she let her eyes meet his, that storm would become a hurricane, causing chaos in her world.

'Lynsey?'

Her head turned quickly, questioningly. She saw the good cut and fabric of the dark suit he wore as comfortably as if it were a part of him. There was an enigmatic air about him. Did it, she wondered, arise from his intellect, or was it an offshoot of his lifestyle and his status in the world?

Her friend's brother he might be, but her intuition told her that he lived in a milieu of which she had no experience or knowledge. Nor would she ever, she reflected, but oh, the joy if she could!

'The one you ran away from,' Madoc asked, raising his glass to his mouth and watching her over its rim, 'is he your boyfriend?'

'If you mean Des, he's a colleague, one of our group.'

He put his glass down. 'So the field's clear?'

There was an excited leap in her chest. 'For—for whom?'

His hand moved towards her shoulder and she did not draw back. He picked off a piece of confetti, holding it up. 'Is this prophetic, an omen?'

Lynsey laughed, shaking her head. 'Boyfriends come, boyfriends go, but no one special.' Until today ... The thought came so loud and clear she thought he must have heard it.

He watched the tiny, circular piece of paper descend.

'You're the next,' Lynsey joked.

His gaze hit hers. 'Oh?' He had withdrawn a little of himself. 'You know something I don't?'

Her smile faltered but re-established itself. 'I had it on the authority of the little bridesmaid, a niece of yours. She told me her mother said so.'

He nodded and his good humour seemed restored. 'The family is irritated by my single state. They've done their best to pair me off, but most of their offerings are burnt.' He leaned back, looking at her narrowly and taking a drink.

'You——' Lynsey took a drink, too. 'You sound very arrogant.'

He looked surprised, then laughed, head back. People turned to stare and seemed to be speculating, is this the happy couple, after all?

'Not arrogant,' he corrected, still amused, 'merely factual.' He gave her a sidelong glance. 'I could elaborate, I could compare your freshness with their stale taste, but I won't. Like another drink? No?' He put out his hand. It was a long-fingered hand, yet capable. And as far as Lynsey was concerned, irresistible. 'It's time for my reward for finding your shoe.'

His words confused her, making her colour. 'I told you, I didn't mean it. I was simply trying to cheer my friends up.'

His brows rose. 'They needed that, at a wedding?'

'They couldn't throw off their worries, so I tried to create a diversion. We work for Lantern Scientific. I expect you've heard the name, since Morwenna works for them, too?'

His eyes were on her face as if it interested him far more than anything she might be saying. Lynsey wondered if he were truly listening.

'There's talk of a takeover,' she told him. 'More than talk. They're worried about their jobs. So am I, but,' she added brightly, 'I'm trying not to let it spoil my enjoyment of life.'

The laughter lines around his eyes crinkled. 'Wise girl.' His hand came out again, resting on hers. 'I'm still waiting.'

'I'm not going home,' she insisted. 'I told you, I've booked a room at this hotel.'

'So have I.' He pulled a key from his pocket. 'Room five. What's yours?'

'It's—I've forgotten.'

He pulled her up. 'Let's find out, shall we?'

The woman at reception said, 'Good evening, Mr Morgan,' and, with a friendly smile, handed Lynsey her key.

'Number eight,' said Lynsey, holding it up.

'Opposite mine.'

Madoc took her hand and Lynsey threw an anxious glance in the receptionist's direction, wondering if she had heard, but the woman was answering a phone call.

'Mr Morgan,' Lynsey said, trying to free her hand, 'it was a joke I had with the others. I honestly didn't mean it literally.' They were climbing the stairs and she strained to look behind her but saw no wedding guests hovering. 'What will your relatives think?' He did not answer. They were past the turn at the top. 'Mr Morgan, I don't want anyone to think I'm that kind of——'

'All I'm doing is taking you to the equivalent of your home.' His tone was so neutral, Lynsey's cheeks burned. All the same, his eyes held a very masculine desire.

'Thank you for that.' She waited for him to go.

He turned her towards the door marked eight, took her key and used it. He stood in the doorway and she looked up at him, her eyes ensnared by his.

'Well?' he said softly.

'Yes?' was her whispered answer.

He took a forward pace and the door clicked behind him. He reached out and plucked something from her hair.

She laughed shyly. 'More confetti?'

'Stardust.' He held up a tiny silver star shape, then watched as it floated down. His hands closed on her upper arms. 'It's in your eyes, too, Lynsey.' He drew her against him and her head tilted back. There was only the light from the sunset, but she saw the warmth in his features, the sensual fullness of his lips.

There was something else in his face, all mixed up with the rest, and Lynsey wished with all her heart that she could identify it.

'You're beautiful,' he said on a whisper, 'you're irresistible, you're——' he eased her away, searched her features, eased her back, 'compulsive loving.' His mouth fixed over hers, gently prising open her lips. She felt his kiss invade and penetrate and knew that it was right. She gave him greater access and her nerves tingled, her legs grew weak.

Gradually he withdrew and she stared up at him wonderingly. 'How——' she cleared her husky throat, 'how has this happened? Something's hit me and I haven't even had time to duck. I—I——' the smile went, came back, 'I didn't even want to.'

'Don't try and analyse,' he cautioned, trailing his fingers around her throat. 'It would be like tearing——' he nodded towards the darkening windows, 'the sunset to pieces.'

'Sunrise,' she prompted, staring up at him in wonderment, thinking, what other man would show such sensitivity to so common a phenomenon as the setting sun? 'There's hope in the sunrise, as well as beauty. I'm a morning-time woman,' she told him, laughing and putting up a hand to push back his hair, but drawing it back quickly.

He saw the uncertain movement and smiled. He had no similar inhibition about touching her and fitted his hand round her nape, letting her hair flow over it.

'Will I,' he asked, 'see this woman's face reflecting the sunrise—its hope, its promise of a new day?' He tipped back her head and minutely examined her features. 'A new life?'

'Madoc, I don't know what you're saying. I—I'm not . . . It's all too fast.'

He pressed her head against him and she closed her eyes at the pleasure, the excitement, the *rightness* of the contact. 'Do you want me to slow the pace,' he asked roughly, 'to stand back and let you escape? Because it would kill me to see you go.' The words vibrated in his chest beneath her forehead.

'Madoc,' she stirred against him, 'I want time, please give me time.'

He released her abruptly, saying, 'Good night, Lynsey.' She watched him open the door and walk away and her heart trotted after him. 'Where are you going?' She had not meant to ask, but all of her had tensed in an effort to hold him back.

The whole lean line of him turned and Lynsey thought for a crazy moment that he was going to rejoin her, but he stayed where he was. 'For a walk in the grounds, then to bed. Why?'

She couldn't tell him, I thought you might get into your car and go, I thought I was going to lose you for ever. So she lifted her shoulders, pretending non-chalance. 'I just wondered.' She closed the door before she gave away any more of her feelings.

So many hours, she thought, until morning. She moved to the window and stared out into the moonlit darkness in which he was walking. How long since I met him, she thought, a few hours? It's like half a lifetime. It seemed she had known him all her life. He was the one who was her man in her dreams, the handsome hero she had conjured up even in her early teenage romanticising; the one she had half-consciously been looking for without ever acknowledging that such a man could in reality exist.

He came into her dreams that night, but she never got to touch him. The more she reached out, the more elusive he became, putting himself beyond her fingers' tips and laughing at her cruelly when she cried out that she wanted him to love her.

The first birds' cries awoke her and she pattered to the window, eyes lifting to the distant mountains of Wales. This, she thought, is the land where he was born. It's a beautiful country with its green fields and rising hills, the music in its landscape, its rock-strewn, rugged summits. Besides his parents' influence, she reflected, it must have played a part in forming his early character, with its valleys and its solitude, its moorland and its wild shores.

Looking at her watch, she saw that daylight was barely an hour old. No one else was stirring and it was too early to dress, so she went back to bed. Lying on her side, she watched the curtains moving in the breeze, thinking about the man who slept just across the corridor.

Was I wrong, she wondered, to let him go last night, when everything inside me was saying, let him stay? How would she be feeling now if she had? Not empty, like I do now, she thought, not half-alive and listless. As she lay there, the wave of longing which swept through her mind and her body, not just for Madoc Morgan's love, but for everything about him, became so strong she had to clench her hands and squeeze her eyes shut to control its rising beat.

The bedroom door creaked. She turned, startled, unbelieving, watching it open. Madoc was there, shirt loosely open over creased trousers, his hair still vaguely damp from showering. He closed the door softly and stood regarding her, holding up a key.

'If you want to know, I took it last night.' He tossed it on to a chair.

'But why?' The words came hoarsely from a mouth suddenly dry.

'I intended to return. You wanted time, I've given you time.'

'Oh, Madoc,' she lifted herself on to an elbow, 'I—I'm not sure . . . I don't know . . .'

He sat sideways on the bed. 'You knew.' He pulled her against him, pressing her cheek to his chest. He stroked her hair. 'You knew, as I did, the moment we saw each other.' He eased down the narrow strap of her nightgown and pressed his lips to the smooth skin of her shoulder. 'I knew how you'd feel to my touch, I knew how you'd taste, how sweet your scent would be if I breathed you in.' He inhaled against her throat. 'That perfume——'

'It's my own, me—real, nothing added.' She tried to laugh, but it was shaky. 'Madoc——' She drew away, looking into his face. 'I've known you—No, that's not correct. I don't know you—I met you yesterday about five o'clock.' She saw the intenseness in his eyes, the tautness around his features, traced the sensitivity of his lips, the strong chin. 'No, that's not true, either.'

He hauled her into a kneeling position on the bed and fastened his arms around her middle. Her arms went round his shoulders and her face rested against his hair.

Closing her eyes, she said, 'I've known you for years, the man I've dreamed about since I knew such a thing as love between the sexes existed. Oh, Madoc, Madoc,' her cheek found his, pressing against it, 'my upbringing tells me it's wrong, but all my instincts say it's right. Which should I believe?'

He was so still she moved a little to look at him. His

jaw had firmed, his body was rigid. He was not forcing her, he was waiting!

'My shoe,' she laughed tremulously, 'it all began with that. I——' she caught her breath, 'I—Please,' her eyes sought his and she made a gesture of helplessness, 'I'm in a strange land, lost, Madoc.'

'But no stranger, Lynsey.' His voice was low. 'Nor am I. I'm Morwenna's brother, not just a man passing by. Doesn't that give you confidence in me?' He spoke gently and his hand came out, touching her breast through the silky material. Her flesh started to burn, and when he slipped the top down, revealing the rounded fullness, her arms reached out.

'Will you guide me,' she whispered, 'show me the way?'

A light leapt into his eyes, then his mouth came down blotting out all thought, all reason, all doubt. He peeled away the thin nightdress, holding her from him, looking at her.

'Remove my shirt, Lynsey,' he instructed. 'Now learn about me as I'm learning about you. Memorise me, just as I'm committing you to memory. The softness, the beauty of you . . .'

Impulsively, her lips pressed against his chest, the soft hairs scratching at her nose and making her wrinkle it. His face came alive as he witnessed her happiness and he scooped her around the waist, lifting her the better to caress her breasts with his tongue, moving downwards, his lips bringing her to a state of breathless longing.

Soon, he was naked as she was and she felt the rough friction of his thighs against hers, his chest hairs scraping her breasts, his hard arousal making her hold still, keeping back her breath.

He stilled his movement, too, and his desiring eyes

sought the anxiety in hers. 'Doubts, my love?' he queried softly. 'You wish me to hold off, give you more time?'

Her gratitude for his forbearance, his understanding and his self-control rushed into her eyes and she felt them moisten. 'No, no, Madoc, I trust you like I've trusted no other man. And,' she reached up to whisper, 'I *want* you like I've wanted no other man before you. I want you to be the first. Madoc?'

She was asking him now and his mouth was all over hers, then, when her whole body was aching for him, she felt him take her, with a gentleness that deepened her gasps and minimised the resulting pain. She felt his possession with joy, her hands gripping his shoulders.

'Give me all of yourself,' he urged, 'come, my lovely, hold nothing back.'

And she gave him herself in her entirety, all of her doubts behind her.

When it was over, they lay entwined. After a while, he said, 'I'm not letting you go. I want you to marry me. And,' he pushed her chin upwards, searching her features, 'don't tell me it's too soon. You know, as well as I know, that it's right between us on every level. *Wnei di fy mhriodi i?* Will you marry me?'

'But, Madoc,' her eyes closed to escape from the temptation in his. 'I'm—I'm bad-tempered sometimes, I get angry about things, I snap at people, especially in the mornings.'

He was laughing, his eyes loving her features, his hands caressing her hips, her breasts. 'So what's terrible about those characteristics? I'm like a bear at times, quite unbearable, I'm told. Ask Morwenna. Does that make you hate me?'

Lynsey laughed, then sighed. 'It makes no difference, Madoc, to this feeling I have for you. It rises above everything. I—I think I could stand your unbearableness just as long as you——' she snuggled against him, 'hold me like this every night.'

'I think I can guarantee that,' he answered. 'So, my love, you're saying "yes"?'

'Yes, yes, Madoc. Oh, Madoc,' she rolled her forehead against his middle, 'I never guessed I could ever be so happy or that life could be so wonderful.' She stared at him. 'In fact, it's so wonderful, it worries me.'

'Will this make you feel more secure?' Momentarily, he removed his arms, then took her left hand and pushed a ring on to her wedding finger. 'It was my grandfather's. My own father gave it to me. I want you to wear it until we choose another.'

'I'll cherish it,' she assured him, holding it to her.

'I've given you part of me,' he said, easing her against him, his palm feathering her back. 'Part of my family, part of my past. Now do you see how much I think of you?'

'After such a short time . . .' She shook her head, her hair spread across his ribs. 'I still can't take it in.' Her ear picked up the strong beat of his heart. With her finger, she traced his hairline, his tapered brows, his resolute jaw. He moved his hands to spread them over the inward curve of her waist, moving up to span her ribcage. Her breath came quickly as a throb of longing took her by surprise.

'I want you again, Lynsey.' His eyes stayed on her face as he cupped her breasts, moving his thumb around their hardened points.

'Oh Madoc, I——' She shook her head and the tiny seeds of doubt which had started to take root scattered and vanished. Her fingers found his ribs, but her touch was shy and soft, yet seemed to excite his desires still more.

His mouth swooped to capture the swelling softness and she gave a gasp of choked delight. He played her body as a musician plays an instrument, putting music into her mind and a rhapsody into her deepest being.

He moved on to her then, letting her know of his own deep desire.

'Madoc, I—I love you,' she heard herself say, and with the tiny fragment of her mind that had any reasoning left in it, she thought, Can that be true? Do I love him after knowing him for less than a day? It was true, she thought dreamily, powers of reasoning finally giving way to the incoming tide of emotion, from the moment I saw him. Again, her pulses hammered as she felt the burning pressure of him easing into the most intimate part of her.

Her cry was a sigh, short and muffled. He captured it with his mouth as the mixing of their bodies created an immense canvas of colour in her mind and a singing pleasure in the heart of her. She heard herself repeating his name, over and over, as if it were itself a promise of lifelong faithfulness.

'My Lynsey,' he muttered against her throat, his body still possessing hers, 'my wife. You're mine, you understand?'

There was a wildness in his look as he lifted his head and stared deep into her eyes. 'I pledge myself to you. The legal ceremony will come soon, but you're bound to me now.'

'I'm bound to you, Madoc,' she echoed, mesmerised by his blazing gaze.

He moved from her and reached out to pull at a cover, then turned her into him. As she slipped into a deep and wonderful sleep, Lynsey thought, he's bound to me, too. Why didn't he say so?

When they woke again, all her doubts were forgotten. He was still there beside her and that was all that mattered.

Lying in his arms, she shared her pillow with him. He was awake, looking at her, yet she had the strangest feeling he was not seeing her. Panic hastened her heartbeats as she fought like a tigress with the possibility that he had been dreaming of another woman all the time he had slept beside her.

His eyes were focused on her now, his smile warming, melting her fears. He reached for her mouth, caressing it with his, then using his tongue to part her lips. The kiss deepened, their limbs entangled, but he had plainly not intended to carry the lovemaking through. Holding her away, he let his gaze wander over her reclining form.

Her instinct was to cover herself, but there was another feeling overtaking it—of wanting to tell him, keep looking at me that way because it burns me up with a loving desire. Her fingers rubbed at his upper lip, sliding to his chin. He smiled and let her play.

'You're a stranger,' she asserted, watching her moving hand to avoid meeting his eyes.

'A stranger, although I've made love to you?'

She nodded, concentrating now on the long straightness of his nose. 'I've let you come closer to me than any other man, yet I still feel you're a stranger.'

At last her eyes found courage, seeking his after the challenge she had thrown him, but they ricocheted from the sudden chilling remoteness in his. It was gone as quickly as a snowflake melting on a warm palm.

'Time will cure that,' he answered, running his hand over her from shoulder to thigh, 'plus our increasing familiarity with each other's ways and thoughts.'

Lynsey nodded, sighing happily.

They were late down to breakfast. A swift glance around the dining room revealed that there was no one there that Lynsey knew, nor it seemed, did Madoc.

A waiter directed them to a table beside a picture window. It framed the magnificent view beyond it and Lynsey could not tear her eyes from the landscape it encapsulated. The beauty of the mountains, great though it was, was heightened still more by the wonder and joy that bubbled through her body and sparkled in her eyes.

She looked at the signet ring on her finger, then at the man who had given it to her. 'Am I dreaming?' she asked.

'If you are, then I'd better be in it.'

Smiling, she twisted the ring. 'I—I hope you're not just a dream.'

'Feel me.' He put his hand across the table. When hers met his, his fingers closed over them and lifted them to his lips.

Her colour heightened and her eyes scanned the room.

'We're not being watched, if that's what you're afraid of,' he commented. 'Most of my family seems to have risen early and gone. Are any of your colleagues here?'

Lynsey shook her head. 'Morwenna booked me in here at her own expense. The others from work couldn't afford to stay the night. Anyway, they're all too anxious about their immediate future to spend too long enjoying themselves.' With a bright smile, 'If you know what I mean.'

'Not exactly.' There was a question in his voice.

Her shoulders lifted and fell. 'The man at the head of the company that's gobbling us up has a terrible reputation.'

He made a face and Lynsey laughed. 'In what way?' he asked. 'Characterwise? Maybe he's a muddler, doesn't know his job?'

'Worse,' she answered. 'He's too good at it. Cuts out waste regardless of the human suffering involved. An employee is just a statistic to him, not a person. We're all dreading it.'

'So if he puts his nose round your company's door, there'll be trouble?' His eyes were on her lips now.

'Big trouble.'

He reached out to flick a stray curl. 'And you'll be in the front line of the rebellion?'

'I'll lead it,' she declared, then laughed, the stars back in her eyes.

The waiter took the order and, aware of Madoc's eyes upon her, Lynsey moved the shining cutlery around. The white of the tablecloth and the rosy pink of the smaller cloth set diagonally across it found an echo in the delicate pink and grey of the striped wallpaper. There was almost a bridal touch to the atmosphere and Lynsey's heart leapt at the thought.

Her fingers felt instinctively for the ring and her eyes lifted to meet Madoc's. 'Tell me again—you did ask me to marry you, didn't you?'

'Forgotten already?

She shook her head. 'Just making sure again that I'm not dreaming.'

He smiled and drank the fruit juice which the waiter had put in front of him. There was a call across the room and Madoc looked at the group of people who had come in, raising his hand but making no attempt to converse with them.

'Relatives of yours?' Lynsey asked, feeling their eyes on her.

'Friends of the family.'

Lynsey nodded, gazing out at the panoramic view of hills and fields and receding valleys which the picture window framed as though it were an inspired painting.

'Tell me about your work,' Madoc encouraged with a smile, and Lynsey lifted her shoulders.

'Seems like it's another world at this moment, plus all the worries about the future connected with it.' She spread some toast with marmalade. 'I work in the research department of Lantern Scientific. David—my brother—he works in the same department. And Sam Wilkinson; also Des Parsons——'

'Des. He was the one who was so anxious you shouldn't come with me?'

Lynsey smiled. 'That's right. He thinks he and I have got—well, an understanding.'

'And you haven't?' Lynsey shook her head decisively. 'When are you going to put him out of his misery?'

'Next time I see him, I'll show him this.' She held up the ring, then sighed. 'I still can't believe this has happened. Tell me again, Madoc—you did ask me to marry you, didn't you?'

'I asked you to marry me,' he answered patiently, and poured coffee for them both. He held up his cup. 'To Lynsey, my wife-to-be.'

Lynsey reciprocated. 'To you, Madoc. And to Morwenna, wherever she is, for having such a wonderful brother.' Carefully, she returned her cup to the saucer. 'What about your work, Madoc?' she asked, putting her hand over his as it rested on the table.

His eyes glinted. 'Would you still marry me if I told you I was an unknown artist living in a basement?'

Lynsey's response was immediate and unhesitating. 'I wouldn't care what you were, or if you'd been unemployed for years, I'd still marry you.'

It took him a few moments to answer, 'I'm a business man. My work takes up a great deal of my time.' His smile flashed at her and her heart jumped with happiness. 'Hobbies varied, both outdoor and indoor.'

Lynsey rested her chin on her clasped hands and stared at him, her love in her eyes. 'Do you travel the world?'

'When my work calls for it.'

There was a slight commotion at the entrance. Madoc looked up and a man called, *'Bore da, Madoc.'*

Madoc lifted his hand, his eyes narrowing slightly. A woman looked at Lynsey, then spoke to Madoc across the room in a language Lynsey could not understand. Madoc glanced at her and replied. The three people nodded and, still looking at Lynsey, took their seats at a table.

'That was Welsh?' Lynsey asked and Madoc nodded. 'Are they your relatives?' He nodded again. 'Long lost?'

'Lost enough to want to catch up on my private life,' he commented succinctly.

'I guess they were asking about me?' He didn't answer. 'Did you tell them?'

'No.' He pushed back his seat. 'Ready? Then let's go.'

He took a route to the exit which put a dozen tables between himself and his relatives. All the same, Lynsey knew they were looking at her all the way to the door.

In the bedroom, Madoc cupped her face, his eyes seeming to kiss each piquant feature. 'Stay this way,' he said huskily. 'I love your laughing eyes, your beauty——'

'I'm not beautiful, Madoc,' she whispered, 'not really.'

He shook his head, as if irritated by her denial. 'It's everything about you, the charm you're not even aware you've got, the intelligence in your face.'

His arms brought her against him and his lips played with hers until they parted, allowing him to enter and taste and explore. She wrapped her arms around his neck, tightening them as the feeling came over her yet again that it wasn't real after all. It had all happened in her mind, it was a daydream . . .

It was, she was certain, the sounds of the outside world intruding and making her unsure: of car doors slamming, of people calling 'goodbye', of reality. It was that other lifetime she had lived, before yesterday, before Madoc, that was hammering at the doors of her mind, and there was nothing she could do now to hold it back.

They went down the staircase hand in hand, Madoc carrying Lynsey's suitcase as well as his own. Earlier, he had settled both hotel bills, saying that, as Morwenna's brother, he had every right to do so.

There were people in the entrance foyer. A group stood at reception, others were carrying cases to their cars. A middle-aged couple hurried after a late breakfast in the dining room.

With some apprehension, Lynsey recognised them as Madoc's parents. How would they react, she wondered, to the new familiarity which she and Madoc could not hide. How much would they guess from her appearance, from the brightness in her eyes, the way her hand was linked with Madoc's?

They looked up, smiled, then stared. Although they recovered quickly Mrs Morgan's eyes held a question, one she did not at that moment ask.

'You enjoyed the wedding, dear?' she said, addressing Lynsey, but did not wait for an answer. She looked at their linked hands. 'You knew Madoc before yesterday?'

Lynsey glanced up quickly, wondering how to answer, seeking a sign in Madoc's face. None was there. 'Morwenna sometimes talked about him,' she replied, avoiding a direct lie. Well, she silently justified the assertion, Morwenna had—once. He was, she had said, at thirty-three, eight years older than herself.

'You can stop searching on my behalf, Mother,' Madoc said without expression. 'I've found her.'

'Found who, dear?' Mrs Morgan answered, looking a little strained. 'But what about Monique——?'

'Now isn't that nice,' Mr Morgan broke in, heartily. 'And right and proper, too, in a way. You'll be able to boss her about properly from now on, won't you, son?'

'What do you mean, Mr Morgan?' Lynsey asked, frowning and removing her hand from Madoc's hold.

'He's going to be your new boss. Didn't you know that, dear? Or didn't Morwenna tell you?'

CHAPTER TWO

LYNSEY stared through the window of her two-roomed flat, looking at but not seeing the line of suburban gardens stretching to the right and left of the two-storeyed early twentieth-century house in which she lived.

She sighed, looking at her hands. The ring Madoc had given her had not been on her finger long enough to make even the slightest imprint. It had all been a dream, after all, she thought unhappily, recalling the harshness of their parting.

Madoc's parents had gone on their way. He had said, 'Well?' and Lynsey had gone cold. In their short acquaintance, he had never once used that tone to her.

'I'm sorry,' she had answered and had begun tugging at the ring.

He grasped her wrist and propelled her into the empty television lounge, closing the door. 'You're sorry, are you? What about?' There had been such a chill in his tone, matching the temperature of his eyes, that Lynsey had shivered.

'It's over,' she answered, managing to control the trembling of her lips. 'Not that it had ever really begun, had it? A couple of hours in bed with me——' She shook her head then went on, feeling tears threaten but managing to keep them in their place. 'It didn't merit a proposal of marriage, Mr Morgan, nor presenting me with what you implied was something of a family heirloom.'

It came off at that moment and she thrust it back at him. He did not take it, so she pushed it into his pocket, withdrawing her hand as if it had been burnt by the close contact.

'Tell me something,' he said, folding his arms and looking so reasonable that she began to feel reassured. But she was certain that underneath that apparent impassivity anger seethed. 'What's so different about myself as your lover and myself as the man who, in a few days, will be head of the company for which you work?'

'Do you really not know? As the man who—who made love to me, you were my equal. As my employer, you're in a different world.'

'Marry me and you'll be part of that world.'

'It's not just your world. It's—it's you, your character.' Yes, she thought, there's the anger, sitting in his eyes like a tiger about to spring. All the same, she went on, head high, 'All the things I've heard about you, the way you don't care how much your decisions hurt your employees, the—the way you sack them without any compunction——'

She swayed as his hand came out, shrank back as it grasped her shoulder, gasped as she hit the hard wall of his body. When his other hand spread around the back of her head, holding it rigid, she gasped.

His mouth ground against hers, and as his teeth punctured her inner lips, she whimpered and struggled for breath, tasting the salt of her own blood. His kiss was denying her the right to breathe, even to stand as she felt her legs grow weak. Her hands found his arms and his body became her only support.

When her fingers slid up and around to press against his neck, she realised her lips were giving him

back all his kisses, and she knew that the whole
process of loving was starting again. She tore herself
away and made for the door.

Seizing her suitcase, which Madoc had dropped to
one side of the entrance foyer, she ran outside. A
glance over her shoulder told her that he was staring
after her, but there was no warmth in his gaze, only a
thinly veiled fury. Probably, Lynsey thought bitterly,
no woman had ever run out on him before.

Someone called out, 'Like a lift to the station,
dear?'

The woman, Lynsey recognised, had been a
wedding guest. 'Oh yes, please,' Lynsey had answered,
and scrambled into the car.

It was over three weeks now since the wedding, time
in which Lynsey had attempted to forget she had ever
met a man called Madoc Morgan but, no matter how
hard she had tried, she had not been able to get him
out of her mind.

At work, David, her brother, had often glanced her
way but had made no comment. Carole, his fiancée,
had asked, 'Everything okay, Lynsey?'

Lynsey's bright smile had carried conviction.
'Couldn't be better,' she had answered. Behind her
back, Lynsey had crossed her fingers. There was a
secret she hadn't told anyone—a secret that was
making her almost sick with fear.

Back from her honeymoon, Morwenna burst into
the research department looking for Lynsey. They
hugged each other and Lynsey exclaimed, 'You look
great. Is marriage really that wonderful?'

If there was a note of wistfulness in Lynsey's voice,
Morwenna did not pick it up.

'Lynsey, it's terrific! You should try it some time.'

She paused and stared. 'You don't look very great yourself.'

'I'm fine,' Lynsey assured her just a little too quickly, but again Morwenna did not notice.

'Doing anything on Saturday week?' she asked. 'Griff and I are having a barbecue. A few friends, his, mine . . . okay? Come around seven.'

As she made to go, Lynsey challenged impulsively, 'Why didn't you tell me about your brother?'

Morwenna frowned again. 'You mean about his company swallowing up ours? He told me not to mention it, not to anyone here, not even my friends. Sorry, Lyn. But, at the wedding, I did try to warn you.'

Lynsey sighed, nodding. 'Thanks for that.'

'Look, Lyn——' Morwenna seemed concerned. 'I don't know how involved with him you are, but——' She shook her head and Lynsey's heart dived. 'He's the biggest charmer I know. People say we're alike but——' she sighed, 'I haven't got his terrific eyes, his looks. Lynsey, he mesmerises people, gets them to do things, well—almost against their will.'

Lynsey gritted her teeth, then nodded, knowing exactly what Morwenna meant. Hadn't he mesmerised her, convinced her he'd meant it when he'd called her 'my love', and that she was already his 'wife', even saying—her heart gave a painful throb—that it would kill him to see her go away. Yes, she thought, I know just what Morwenna means.

'Well,' Morwenna went on, 'there's another side to him. His charm's only skin deep. You don't have to dig very far to find how hard he can be. Where his work's concerned, he lets nothing—absolutely nothing—stand in his way.'

'I—I met your mother after the wedding,' Lynsey

remarked, examining her finger where Madoc's ring had been. 'She said something about someone called Monique.'

Morwenna nodded. 'She's the daughter of some friends of theirs. We're expecting Madoc to announce his engagement to her any time now.' There was compassion in her eyes as she glanced at Lynsey. How much had she guessed? Lynsey wondered.

Morwenna looked at the office clock. 'Remember Saturday.' She lifted her hand. 'See you around some time.'

Lynsey glanced left and right, feeling as empty inside as the corridor in which she stood after watching Morwenna leave. Who am I looking for? she thought, and before she could find an answer her heart leapt. A man had turned the corner and was coming towards her.

'Lynsey.' His eyes brightened, appreciating her looks, her femininity. 'I couldn't get to Morwenna's wedding. How was it?'

Her heartbeat resumed its normal rhythm. How could I fool myself so? she reproached herself. How could I have been so stupid as to let my dreams encroach so much into my everyday thoughts?

This man's eyes weren't brown and warm, his hair did not have the dark sheen she had been looking for; his eyebrows were not an emphatic curve, nor was there the deep intelligence in his face that Madoc Morgan's possessed.

'It was fun, Sam. The bride was beautiful——'

'They always are.' Sam Wilkinson's mouth smiled but there was a bitterness in his tone which prompted Lynsey to examine his face. Had he, she wondered, quarrelled with his wife again?

'Sam,' she had to ask him, 'have you heard the

news? The head of the company that's taking us over is Morwenna's brother.' His slight hesitation told her that he had. 'But then you would know, I suppose. You and Bill—you started Lantern Scientific, didn't you?'

His shoulders lifted and dropped. 'It was unavoidable, Lynsey. We were offered a good price——' He glanced at his watch. 'Do you have lunch in the staff canteen?'

'Sometimes,' Lynsey answered.

'Good. Keep a seat for me today, will you?'

Smiling, Lynsey nodded and returned to her desk.

Sam was there first, standing by a table, looking for her among the crowd. He lifted his hand as she came in.

Lynsey nodded, collected her meal and made her way across the bright, airy canteen.

Sam pulled out a chair, waiting until Lynsey had settled. He joined her, wrapping his hands around his cup as if, instead of a glowing day in May, it was midwinter and he needed the warmth. He looked drawn, Lynsey noted, wondering which of his own particular problems was worrying him most.

'Was it so terrible, Sam,' Lynsey hazarded, eating her meal without much enthusiasm, 'being taken over after all the work you've put into the company?'

Sam looked up, eyes dull, mind plainly elsewhere. 'Sorry?' he asked absently.

So it's not that, Lynsey concluded, pushing her half-empty plate away. It's his move now. She watched his bent head, his auburn hair falling forward as he studied his coffee revolving in the cup. His round face carried lines of strain, his shirt was creased under a well-worn jacket. He did not look the accomplished young business man any more, and Lynsey's heart went out to him.

'Something wrong?' Lynsey probed gently. There had to be a reason, she guessed, why he had sought her out.

Sam ran a hand over his forehead. 'Everything's wrong.' He looked at her intently. 'Didn't you know? My wife left me a few weeks ago. She took Terry, our young son with her.'

'I'm so sorry,' Lynsey replied, feeling inadequate. What could she say in the circumstances? 'So you're having to look after yourself?'

'That's the least of it. I miss her, Lynsey, and I miss my son. I want them back, but——' He made a hopeless gesture.

'Maybe there's another man involved?' she hazarded, yet not wishing to intrude.

He lifted his shoulders as if they were weighted. 'Who knows?' He finished his coffee and lowered the cup to the inner circle on the saucer. 'I don't want to make it a legal matter. Not yet.' He stared into the empty cup. 'I wish I knew what I'd done. I wish she'd told me instead of just walking out.'

Lynsey shook her head, feeling deep sympathy, yet not knowing what to say.

'How can I defend myself,' Sam went on, 'or put things right if I don't know what crime I've committed?'

'Hi, Lynsey.' Des Parsons joined them, pulling out a chair and glaring at Sam Wilkinson as if he had no right to be there. 'Heard the news? The guy that's taking us over—you know, the one you called an inhuman robot—turns out to be none other than Morwenna's brother. Can you beat that?' He pushed half a sandwich into his mouth, chewed and stared at Sam again.

'If you're implying,' Sam said patiently, pushing

away his half-empty plate, 'that you should have been informed of the chairman of Techno-Global's identity, then I'm sorry, Des, but Mr Morgan expressly wished us to keep quiet about it.'

Des tutted and tossed his head and went on eating.

'I expect,' Lynsey put in, hoping to soothe Des's feelings, 'he wanted to protect Morwenna.'

'What from,' Des asked morosely, 'our uncomplimentary remarks—to put it politely—about his vicious methods of running a company?'

'Des,' Sam pointed out long-sufferingly, 'we know nothing about his methods yet, do we?'

'Do we, heck!' Des exclaimed, swallowing some coffee. 'Ask Lynsey's brother—ask him to tell you about the guy Morgan fired with a wife and three-and-a-half kids. And that secretary he sacked with an invalid husband.'

Sam shifted uncomfortably. 'Management decisions, Des. The chairman of an international concern like Techno-Global wouldn't——'

'Wouldn't heck! He did. Chairman's orders, they said.' He shifted to stare reproachfully at Lynsey. 'You knew all that, didn't you, yet you went off with him at the wedding. I watched you go.'

It was Lynsey's turn to shift in her seat. 'I didn't know who he was, then, Des. If I had, I can assure you I wouldn't have gone anywhere with him for a fortune.' The bitterness was almost palpable and she was conscious of Sam's curious glance, but Des seemed unaware of any undercurrent.

Sam pushed back his chair. 'I'll be in touch, Lynsey?'

Hearing the question and sensing the uncertainty, Lynsey smiled and nodded.

Des watched him walk away. 'He's married,' he said bluntly.

Lynsey laughed, keeping Sam's misfortunes to herself. 'If you keep warning me off all the men I smile at, Des, I'll begin to wonder——'

'You've got such a heck of a nice smile,' Des answered, colouring and pushing at his empty dishes.

'Now, Des,' Lynsey laughed, but in a kindly way, 'you've got a very nice girlfriend of your own.' She saw his expression. 'What's wrong? Has she found another man?'

To her surprise, he coloured again. 'We had an argument and she went off with one of my friends.'

'Oh dear, you have a problem there. Gaye's a very attractive girl.'

'Think I don't know? All the other guys are after her.'

Lynsey shook her head, thinking, I know how you feel. There's a man I—well, he's got someone else, so what's the use of loving him? But even if he were free, he's hard and ruthless towards people below him and I couldn't, but couldn't feel anything even faintly resembling love for a man like that. Could I?

As the days crept by, so Lynsey's fears increased. If there were a child, she thought—and nothing had happened to tell her there was not—it would change the whole of her life, because she would never be able to let it go. But how would I manage, she asked whoever was listening although she knew it was only herself; how would my parents take such an addition to the family?

Two days before the barbecue, Des stood by Lynsey's desk. 'There's a rumour Big Brother's paying us a state visit.'

Lynsey's head came up. 'When? Today?' She put a hand to her cheek and felt its coldness. 'Why?'

Des shrugged. 'To look us over, I guess. Do a head count, mop up the slack, which you said he's famous for.' He slouched over to his desk and the door opened.

Serious brown eyes conducted a swift survey of personnel, unhesitatingly pinpointing the pale, agitated girl who held in her hands a sheaf of complicated mathematical notes.

He nodded to David, then glanced disinterestedly at Des. He turned to talk to Bill Paine, greying-haired and rotund, who, with Sam Wilkinson had built up the company from a two-man team to an establishment of fifty-plus employees.

They were still talking as they went out. Madoc had gone without a single glance back! It was as though I didn't exist, Lynsey thought, imagining up a calendar and counting the days all over again. It's always been on time until now ... It's never been late before, never ...

If only, she reproached herself for the thousandth time, I hadn't acted so thoughtlessly that day. Why didn't I remember what the consequences might be? Why was I so blinded by my feelings, so overwhelmed by Madoc's attractiveness that I forgot everything I'd been taught?

That evening David rang, asking if he and Carole could call. Surprised, because her brother rarely visited her, she agreed, glad to have company to take her mind off her problems. The tension inside her body had taken such a hold, she found it almost impossible to smile any more.

It seemed that David and Carole had brought with them their own set of problems.

'There's a rumour,' David said, sprawling in a chair with a can of beer in his hand, 'we're for the chop.'

The anxiety in his eyes belied his relaxed attitude. 'How can Carole and I save up to get married if we both lose our jobs?'

Lynsey was horrified. 'The whole research department? David, no!'

He nodded, taking a swill from the can.

'So that's why he came round this morning,' Lynsey exclaimed, 'to count people, divide by two and get his guillotine ready.'

'To do his chopping act,' Carole put in, feeling the back of her neck with a rueful smile.

'On both finance and staff,' David finished.

Dismay crept upward along Lynsey's spine. Where Madoc's work's concerned, Morwenna had said, he lets absolutely nothing stand in his way. How well his sister knew him . . .

In the tiny kitchen, Carole helped Lynsey make coffee. 'You okay?' she asked.

'Mm. Why do you ask?' Lynsey answered, pretending surprise.

'You're not okay, are you.' Carole leaned on her elbow on the draining board. 'You look as if any moment you're going to burst into tears.' She reached out and tried unsuccessfully to unclench Lynsey's fist. 'Wow, you're tense! Look, I'm going to be your sister-in-law someday. When we can afford the luxury of marriage and kids. So come on, Lyn, tell me.'

Staring out of the kitchen window, Lynsey told her.

'You're not. You can't be! For heaven's sake, Lynsey. Are you sure?'

'Not sure,' Lynsey whispered, 'but there's nothing, although there should be. It usually happens like clockwork, exactly on time, but—Oh God!' She hid her face. 'I wish I knew what to do.' She started shaking, having to grit her teeth to prevent them from chattering.

'Lyn, you're terribly tensed up. Could it be that?'

'I doubt it. You don't know, you just don't know what happened between us.'

After a moment, Carole said, 'Mind if I tell David?' There was no need. David had heard.

He didn't explode with anger as her father might have done, and Lynsey was grateful for his restraint. But there was no doubting his concern.

'I saw you with him at the wedding,' David said worriedly, 'but I thought nothing of it. Didn't know who he was then, anyway. Lyn, have you told him?'

She shook her head. 'He hasn't been near me. I wasn't really expecting him to call.' Just phoed he might, she thought sadly.

'A bit more thought on his part at the time of the event would have——'

'David, it takes two,' Lynsey broke in. 'I should have had more sense. He—he gave me the option that day, yes or no. I could have said no, couldn't I?'

It had seemed so right at the time, her feelings so powerful, his body, his bearing—everything about him—so seductive. He'd said such wonderful things, promised they would marry, given her a ring—a very special ring . . . Yet, all the time he'd known it could never be.

How could he have misled her so? But didn't she know now that it was in line with his character, his lack of compassion for employees, the swift, merciless dismissal of anyone surplus to requirements?

'He's got someone else,' Lynsey said flatly. 'Morwenna told me—her name's Monique. His family's expecting them to announce their engagement any moment now.'

This time David was angry. 'The miserable——'

'Don't just blame him,' Lynsey urged, her hand on

his arm. She tried a small smile. 'I was there, too.'

After a moment, she added, '*If* there is a child, Mum and Dad will help me.'

'Don't be too sure of that,' David remarked, rising and holding out his hand to his fiancée. The parents are broad-minded to a certain degree, but this——' He lifted doubtful shoulders. He and Carole kissed spontaneously, then Carole looked at Lynsey.

'Sorry about that,' she said. 'It was tactless of us.'

Lynsey's shoulders lifted and dropped like her brother's. 'It's good to see you two so happy.' She stood up, going with them to the door. 'Seems we've all got our problems.'

'If Morgan goes ahead and cuts out research,' David reminded her, 'you'll have lost your job, too.'

'That's right,' Lynsey laughed, her customary sense of humour making a brief appearance, 'cheer me up.' Then his comment hit her. Losing her job—at such a time—and with no regular income, how would she manage?

'Somebody needs to—cheer you up, I mean,' Carole said seeing the worry in her friend's eyes.

'Maybe everything will come right,' Lynsey said, staring unseeingly through the doorway as they left, 'maybe tomorrow, or the next day . . .' Oh, let it be soon, she pleaded silently.

CHAPTER THREE

ON the morning of the barbecue, Lynsey felt her spirits rise a little. Her worries had not gone away— they had in fact intensified, each day being more worrying than the one before—but a kind of recklessness had taken over.

If, she reasoned, her life was on the point of a drastic change, this party of Morwenna's was probably the last event she would enjoy before that change began to manifest itself both to herself and the world in general.

She chose a dress with a fit so close that she knew it might be only a matter of time before circumstances forced her to put it to the back of the wardrobe. It was white and lacy with sleeves that wrapped around her arms and a neckline that curved low both back and front.

Around her neck she clasped some chunky black and white beads, and fixed round, black earrings into place. Using little make-up, she brushed her hair until it shone, then slipped into white sandals. If, she thought defiantly, all the rest are in jeans, it won't bother me.

'You look good,' said Morwenna, welcoming her into the neat, modern house she and Griffith had chosen. 'A bit pale. Different, somehow . . .'

Oh heavens, Lynsey thought, is it showing already, inwardly if not outwardly. Her worries threatened to overtake her, like a great roaring wave, but she fought it back and forced a smile to her face. 'I'm fine, honestly.'

Morwenna looked curiously into Lynsey's face. 'Madoc keeps asking if you've arrived. Is there something between you two I've missed?'

Lynsey's heartbeats skipped over one another. 'Nothing whatsoever, Morwenna,' she declared emphatically. She managed a smile. 'You warned me against him, didn't you?'

'Well, come through. We're in the garden. Like a drink? Sam—Lynsey, Sam's here, too. Sam, get Lynsey a drink, there's a pal. Then come outside whenever you want. Okay?' She hurried away.

'Sam.' Lynsey smiled. 'I never dreamt Morwenna would be so good in the hostess role. Isn't this a pleasant house? How could they afford to buy such a place?'

'I asked the same question. It seems that Morwenna's brother footed the bill.'

'Madoc—I mean, Mr Morgan bought it for them?'

'So Morwenna said.' He smiled. 'Despite the rumours, it appears he has his good side, too. Now, about that drink.'

Lynsey was about to shake her head, but thought, why not? I won't be able to much longer . . . She thanked Sam and lifted the glass. 'To happier times for you.'

He frowned, but said, 'Thanks for that,' and took a drink.

'Have you heard anything?' Lynsey asked, thinking that discussing other people's problems might help to keep her mind off her own.

'Nothing.' He looked around but his eyes were plainly seeing another scene. 'Betsy's not exactly the communicative sort. Towards the end, we hardly exchanged a word. That was the worst part.'

If only, Lynsey thought, I could talk to someone about my troubles as he's talking to me.

'Sometimes,' he confided, staring into his glass, 'she'd get at me through Terry, our son. But most of the time, it was silence between us. I tried to break down the barrier, but I just couldn't get through.'

'Didn't you ever quarrel?' Lynsey queried. 'I'm told that often lets off steam in a marriage.'

'I wish we had. At least we'd have been talking to each other.'

He seemed to return to the present, glancing round, seeing people. Lynsey looked about her, too. There were a handful of familiar faces, people who had been at the wedding, friends of Morwenna's and Griffith's, talking, laughing.

There was one woman who wasn't laughing. Her hair was the deepest black, dressed high over a pale forehead, tied at the back into a tail and swept over one shoulder, resting there provocatively.

Her facial structure was stunning. Her expression told whoever was interested—and Lynsey, for some curious reason, was—that, unike the Lynsey Thorpes of this world, her self-confidence was a stable, unwavering thing.

Lynsey did not know why she shivered, but she did. Turning away, she surveyed the scene. The evening was fine and bright, the sun, in a pearl-blue pre-night sky, turning itself into an orange-coloured ball and descending, but not yet inclined to withdraw completely its light and warmth.

Garden flares, planted like flowers, flamed orange, echoing the sun. The fire under a barbecue was beginning to glow. Someone was clattering dishes on a nearby table. On a trolley stood bottles and glasses, dishes of potato crisps and peanuts.

Sam offered the dish of nuts and Lynsey scooped up

a few, tilting back her head and dropping them one by one into her mouth.

'That's partly satisfied my hunger,' she said, smiling and dusting her hands free of salt.

'Bill's here somewhere,' Sam remarked, looking round.

Lynsey did not follow his eyes. Madoc Morgan was somewhere among the crowd and all she wanted was for him to stay there. The last thing she wanted to do was to draw him with her eyes.

'Morwenna invited Bill, too?' Lynsey commented. 'How nice. That's something I've always liked about Lantern Scientific—the friendliness between management and the employees. You and Bill Paine—you're the most senior of all of us, yet you're both so approachable.'

'Glad you've been happy,' said Sam, smiling.

Lynsey frowned. 'You used the past tense. Have things changed that much?' Sam's non-committal gesture was his only answer. 'There's a rumour,' Lynsey went on, 'that departments are going to disappear—well, the research department, anyway.'

'There certainly are going to be changes,' Sam commented evasively. 'Whether for the better, remains to be seen.'

'So Mr Morgan's reputation as the wielder of scythes among the staff isn't far wrong? Sorry,' Lynsey added, seeing Sam's closed expression, 'I shouldn't have asked that. Look,' she exclaimed, her hand on Sam's arm, 'they've started cooking the food. Mm,' she inhaled, making a pretence of enjoying the fun, 'and that smell's making me ravenous.' Pulling him towards the stove, she said, 'Do you think it's okay if we help ourselves?'

'I can't see Morwenna, but——' He paused and

Lynsey glanced at him. He withdrew his eyes from the distance and smiled. 'Why not just carry on? It certainly looks good.'

Beefburgers and steaks were sizzling on the grid. There were kebabs: chunks of meat and sausages, mixed with tomato pieces and peppers and cheese cubes. Lynsey used tongs to pick up the sizzling concoction, then held the skewer on which the pieces were threaded.

'Here, Sam.' She thrust the kebab towards his mouth. 'I know we should push it all on to a plate, but it's more fun this way. Be careful, it's hot.'

He held her hand to steady it and moved it, with the food, to his mouth, maintaining his hold while he took a bite, smiling at her over the top.

It was the first sign in weeks that Sam had shown of animation and Lynsey was delighted. She laughed at him and raised a kebab of her own to her teeth which were ready and waiting to take a bite. Her eyes roved above it, not really seeing but satisfying her taste buds.

There was a smear of grease on her cheek, a deliciously savoury flavour on her tongue—and her gaze became riveted by two brown, furious eyes staring at her across the garden. They flicked to her companion, then back to her.

Sam, chewing, followed her gaze. 'I saw him just now but I didn't want to spoil your evening by telling you the man you love to hate was here.'

Lynsey tried to swallow, failed, then managed it, but convulsively, then felt she could not eat another mouthful. The laughter in her eyes died a painful death. It was a re-run of their first sight of each other—except that this time, there was hostility humming between them, suspicion and, on his part, downright anger.

Searching for a plate, she deposited the food on to it, wiping her mouth with a paper napkin. Her appetite had gone, her determination to enjoy the party had vanished without trace.

All the fears she had so determinedly suppressed welled up again and the wave of despair towered over her, crashing down and taking the fragile threads of her happiness with it.

If, she told herself, the man across the garden was the father of the child she was almost convinced she was expecting, then she should be running to him and telling him so.

Should I? she agonised. Who else is there to help? Not, I could say, for me but for the sake of . . . He was not standing alone. The dark-haired, slender woman who had so much going for her that Lynsey had shivered at the sight of her, stood beside him, her hand on his arm.

So this was the woman called Monique whom Madoc's mother had mentioned and to whom, according to Morwenna, Madoc was soon to become engaged! However could I hope to compete with such a woman? Lynsey asked herself.

Looking from side to side, she searched for a way of escaping. Was it her imagination, she wondered, or had those garden flares died down, the night sky clouded over, the gentle breeze freshened enough to make one shiver?

'Something wong?' Sam asked. 'You're quite pale. Come inside, or maybe another drink will warm you?'

'Well, Sam,' said Bill Paine, strolling up and joining them, 'enjoying yourself? Lynsey, how are you?'

Bill's smile demanded one in return but Lynsey found it impossible to oblige.

'I thought she looked a bit white,' Sam remarked.

Out of the corner of her eye, Lynsey saw Madoc detach himself from his lady friend's arm and make his way towards them. 'No, no, I'm fine,' she answered quickly, smiling first at Bill, then, more lingeringly at Sam.

He smiled back, commenting, 'Lynsey paid us a compliment, Bill. Said how much she's liked working for us and how she particularly appreciated our friendliness and informality of approach.'

Bill's smile turned benign. 'Nice to hear that.' He took a drink from his glass, then held it up. 'Long may it continue.'

Lynsey frowned, trying to hide her fear at the slow, relentless approach of the tall, lean man called Madoc Morgan. People were detaining him, chatting, laughing, but he came closer with every move.

'Do you think,' she responded with a false brightness, longing to take flight but discovering that she could no more make her feet obey than if they were embedded in a bog, 'it will continue under the new management?'

Bill, rotund, genial and plainly indomitably optimistic, moved back a couple of paces. 'Ask the "new management" himself. Mr Morgan,' the formality, Lynsey noted abstractedly, was there already, 'Miss Thorpe here is wondering whether, under your chairmanship, Lantern Scientific will be the happy, friendly company it's been in the past.'

There was no friendliness in the eyes that rested on Lynsey's face, then, scathingly, skittered over her dress. The hostility she had felt coming at her in waves from across the garden was even more apparent at close quarters.

'I suggest,' Madoc answered, each word a chip of ice, 'that Miss Thorpe waits and sees. If, from now on, she doesn't like the atmosphere at her place of work, she can take the course that's always open to her. She can quit.'

Puzzled, Sam looked from one to the other. Even Bill must have felt the antagonism, since he commented gruffly, 'That's the last thing Sam and I would want her to do. She's a warm and extremely pleasant young lady, not to mention efficient. She'd be a loss to the company.'

'That's very kind of you, Bill,' Lynsey answered with a strained smile, 'but I wouldn't enjoy working in a stiff and formal environment. I'd look for another job.' She turned away, then back. 'Please excuse me, Sam, Bill, M-Mr Morgan,' she said, and swung round to run down some steps which led to the other end of the garden.

Flares shot out orange tongues of flame along each side of the path. She was halfway down it when a hand gripped her arm, swinging her round.

'You're an expert in taking flight,' Madoc grated. 'But this time, there's no lost shoe. You missed a trick there. I might have turned Prince Charming again to your Cinderella, then we'd have been back where we started, wouldn't we?'

'Never,' Lynsey exclaimed. 'We'll never be able to go back to the beginning.'

He stood back, hands in pockets. 'I want to talk to you.'

'No, thank you. We've done all the talking we're ever going to do.' All of her worries rose up again in that great threatening wave, poised and waiting. Was it, she wondered, about to crash down again, taking her with it? 'You can go back to your fiancée now. She's missing you.'

His arm jerked out as if to silence her sarcasm. In a pure reflex action, she stepped back. Her foot hit something rigid and there was a scorching heat around her legs. She cried out and, seconds later, was jerked unceremoniously across the path.

Madoc seized the flare and, upending it, thrust it flame-side down into the earth. The flame went out and he threw the flare aside. Lynsey covered her face with her hands and waited, trembling.

'Come this way.' The order was abrupt and uncompromising. Instead of leading the way back to the party, he impelled her towards a shadowy construction at the garden's end. Grappling with a padlock, he pushed her inside, pulling the door behind them.

They were in a small summer-house. In the flickering illumination of the flares, a wooden bench emerged from the semi-darkness. Nearby was a garden chair, a folded patio umbrella and a plant in a tub of earth.

'Did you get burnt?' he asked. 'Are you hurt?'

Yes to both and in more ways than one, she wanted to answer, but shook her head. 'The flame must have come very near. I felt the heat, but that's all.' She knew Madoc was looking at her but she did not meet his eyes.

She wished her legs did not feel so weak at his proximity, nor her reflexes respond quite so fiercely to the dark, enigmatic shape of him.

In the darting light through the window, the planes of his face took on an angled mystery, his eyes a hypnotic gleam.

'What's Sam Wilkinson to you?'

The question, shot at her from the shadows, hit her sharply, bringing her head up.

'The same as Bill Paine. He's one of my employers.'

'You were flashing "come on" signals to Wilkinson from the moment you set eyes on him this evening.'

So he had been watching her from the start! 'You're quite wrong,' she answered, her voice low and intense. If only he knew how useless it was for her even to think about any other man—not that she wanted to.

'You're saying I shouldn't believe what my eyes tell me is true?'

'I'm saying just that,' she answered, going to the window and staring out. It was better looking into the semi-darkness than into the hard brilliance of his eyes. Would they soften, she wondered, if she told him how, as each day passed, she became even more convinced that she was expecting his child?

She rested her head against the glass, hopelessness washing over her. Now she knew the score of her foolishness and it tasted bitter indeed.

Firm, neutral hands turned her round, then released her. 'I have something to say to you.' His body blocked out the light from the window, creating an impenetrable darkness.

His hands were pushed into his trouser pockets. He walked away, returning slowly. 'It may or may not surprise you,' he said at last, 'but over the past few weeks, you've been very much in my mind.'

Snap, she thought, but her expression gave nothing away. 'I'm flattered, Mr Morgan, but——'

He moved. A bunch of her dress was gathered into his fist. He had pulled her so close she could almost taste the faint tang of alcohol on his breath and see the gold-flecked glitter in his eyes. 'Call me by my surname again and I'll throttle you.'

Lynsey moistened her lips with her tongue tip. 'Madoc, I——' She shook her head and, partially mollified, he let her go. Tidying her dress, she closed her eyes again, feeling the throb in her breasts. His hand had only brushed them but they were aching with an acute awareness of his touch.

A hand stroking her hair brought her head up swiftly. 'When we made love, Lynsey——' His hand was under her chin now. 'I should have asked.' His thumb stroked her lips and the softening of his manner was almost her undoing. 'You were a virgin. Forgive me, but—were you protected?'

Slowly she shook her head. It was why, ever since, she had been so twisted up inside.

'And?'

'Nothing,' she whispered.

'Then we must marry.'

'There's no need,' she answered, 'no need for you to worry.'

'There's every need.'

Her heart leapt at his words but she would not let herself believe he meant what he said.

He must have felt her trembling, since he pulled her against him. Her head drooped, finding itself somehow pressed to his chest. His arms held her loosely and she wished he would turn back into the fiercely passionate man she had known that wonderful day, that unforgettable night.

'I'll marry you,' he said at last. 'I accept the responsibility of the outcome of those few hours we spent together,'

As a declaration of love it was a non-starter. It was the statement of an honourable man, one who had a duty to perform. But it caused Lynsey's heart to pound as if she had been running, made her lift her arms and wrap them around his chest, starting tears of gratitude and utter relief.

He eased her away, gently tipping back her face, looking at her for a long time. Shouts and joking cries filtered in through the crack in the doorway. Someone must have lit a bonfire for the intermittent light brightened the summer-house's interior, casting a glow over the planes and ridges of Madoc's hard and handsome face.

'I like your dress,' he said in a softer tone. 'I like the shape of the woman inside it. I shall like it even more when it becomes obvious to the world that she's going to be the mother of my child.'

'Madoc, what can I say but—thank you for being so honourable and responsible and——' His head lowered, his thumb parted her lips and his mouth took hers.

Her arms lifted to encircle his neck and she felt a need grow inside her to melt into him, becoming one with him once more. But he ended the kiss, disengaging her arms, and her heart sank with disappointment. It had been a betrothal kiss, nothing more.

'The wedding must take place as soon as possible.' He stood in the doorway, staring towards the house and the mingling guests. 'Thursday.' He turned. 'Do you agree?' Lynsey whispered 'yes'. 'I'll clear my diary of commitments for two days. That gives us a four-day break.'

Not a honeymoon, she noted, but a 'break'. She dared not ask where they would go, if indeed they went anywhere. It was a marriage arising out of necessity, not love, Lynsey reminded herself unhappily, at least, not on his part. Whether or not the love she herself had given voice to during their lovemaking had really existed, she told herself that she did not know.

'Monique?' she asked.

'What about her?' he returned with a flash of irritation. 'Monique would be there whether I married you or not.'

So, Lynsey thought sadly, in Madoc's scheme of things, marriage may come and marriage may go, but Monique goes on for ever.

'I—I understand,' Lynsey answered, swallowing a sigh.

He turned to look at her. 'Do you?' he said. 'I wonder.'

CHAPTER FOUR

THAT night, Lynsey telephoned her brother. It was late but she knew he would answer even if he had gone to bed.

'David, Madoc's marrying me.'

His response was so long in coming, she wondered if he was annoyed. 'He is?' He sounded stunned. 'When, Lyn? To both events, I mean.'

'Late autumn. And the wedding's on Thursday. He spoke to me tonight at the barbecue. You're the first to know. He didn't even tell his sister. He wanted to call his parents first—about the wedding not the baby. That's still a secret. David,' her voice wavered, 'tell me I'm doing right. My mind was going round in circles trying to think of a solution. I was going to cope with everything without any help from anyone, but—I was right to accept his offer, wasn't I? For the sake of—of what's to come, I mean.'

'For Morgan junior's sake, Lyn, you were absolutely right.'

Her brother's words made the possibility of her pregnancy into even more of a reality. It came to her suddenly that she had no need to be frightened any more. Instead, she could start looking forward to the future, to something, *someone*, who might one day bind Madoc to her in love, not just duty.

'I'd like you and Carole to come to the wedding, David. It'll be a quiet affair.'

'As long as the boss doesn't fire me for being there.' The irony in the situation must have struck him, since

61

he burst into laughter, making Lynsey smile and relax
a little for the first time in days.

'I 'phoned the parents tonight and invited them to the
ceremony. They were as astonished as you are. And
pleased, too, but they can't come. Dad's off to Denmark
on business and Mum's going with him. They asked if
we could postpone it. I had to tell them "no".'

David chuckled. 'Bet you didn't tell them why.'

'No, I didn't. I knew Mum would take it well but,
for her sake, I didn't want to give Dad any cause to
raise the roof.'

Lynsey waited next day for a telephone call that
never came. It was Sunday and she had told herself, Today, he'll come. There's so much to talk
about . . .

In the end, she pulled on an extra layer, since the
evening was chill, and went for a walk.

Returning home, she wondered where her happiness
had gone. In the wake of Madoc's decision to marry
her, she had been almost euphoric. Now, she
wondered why. But, she reasoned, hadn't her
problems gone, and wasn't this tiny being that might
be inside her going to get a father, something of which
she would never deprive any child?

Next morning, Morwenna burst into the research
department. 'Where is she?' she shouted and flung her
arms round Lynsey's neck. 'Great news!' she
exclaimed. 'I never thought you had it in you—to
break down my brother's barriers, I mean. Honest,
Lynsey, when I saw you with him at my wedding, I
thought, I don't want her to get hurt, but now I can
see I was worrying for nothing.'

The hurt you didn't want me to have, Lynsey
thought sadly, disengaging herself from Morwenna's
embrace, has already been inflicted. I should have

taken your advice, shouldn't I? 'Glad you're pleased,' she said, smiling.

'What's going on?' asked Des, emerging from the main office. 'What's great?'

David pushed past him. 'To put it crudely,' he said with a broad grin, 'my sister's got herself a man. Mind what you say from now on, Des. The big bad boss has taken her in tow.'

'What big bad——' Comprehension dawned. 'Him? Lynsey, say it's not *him*'

'Careful,' David cautioned, still grinning. 'His sister's within earshot, too.'

'What's wrong with him, Des?' Lynsey had meant it as a repudiation of the disbelief in Des's voice but it had come out as a question.

'Wrong? He's the enemy, that's who he is. Our enemy, and you're supposed to be on our side. Now you've gone over to his.'

'Sorry, Des,' Lynsey said gently, 'I'm going to marry him.'

'He'll screw you up,' he protested, unmindful of David's playful, warning gestures towards Morwenna. 'He'll make you wish you'd never been born. You know what kind of a low-down reputation he's got.'

'Des,' Morwenna prodded in a kindly way, 'he's my brother. I know he's hard and quite ruthless where work's concerned, but there's a nice side to him, too.'

Des was deaf to her reasoning.

'For Pete's sake, Lyn, couldn't you have found someone better? There's dozens of men would like to marry a nice girl like you, some of 'em here in this building, and I'm not just talking about me.'

He blushed scarlet at his own declaration and turned away, mumbling, 'That's the end of the research department, folks. Without Lynsey to fight for us, we might as well pack up and go.'

Morwenna made a face. 'My brother's got a wonderful reputation, hasn't he? And there's all our family thinking what a wonderful guy he is because he's a top industrialist and all that.' She grew serious as the others drifted away. 'You do remember I told you about Monique?'

Lynsey nodded, keeping all expression from her face. She couldn't say, Don't worry, he's not pushing Monique out of his life just because he's marrying me. Aloud, she said, 'Will the family be disappointed?'

Morwenna shook her head, bewildered. 'We were so certain he was going to marry her. Her parents and mine are very old friends. Mum and Dad produced one girl after another for Madoc but Monique was the only one he didn't throw overboard.'

The telephone rang and Lynsey, for once, was thankful it was her duty to answer it. It prevented Morwenna from seeing the pain in her eyes.

'See you lunchtime,' Morwenna mouthed from the door. 'Okay?'

Lynsey nodded and took the call. 'Lantern Scientific research,' she said.

'I have a call for you,' a voice sang. 'Mr Morgan from head office.'

Lynsey, hand shaking, lifted the telephone and walked with it to a more private corner. Someone spoke, but plainly not to her. He seemed to be giving orders, finishing a conversation of his own.

'Lynsey?' he said at last. 'I want to see you tomorrow evening, take you out for a meal. Are you free?'

He's making an appointment with me, she thought. The top industrialist fits me, his wife-to-be, into his working life. He's only marrying me because he's so methodical—he wouldn't be where he was, would he, if he weren't?—tidying up his life, filing away odds and ends such as the woman who, through an oversight on his part, just happens to be expecting his offspring.

That is, if I am, she thought—Oh, if only I weren't!

'Will you give me an answer!'

'Oh Madoc, I'm sorry. Yes, yes, I'll be free.' If she said, I can't wait to see you again . . . yesterday was a long day without you . . . why didn't you call? the man at the other end would be angry. He was not the man who had said to her, his eyes alight with passion, It would kill me to see you go. Now, she thought with a silent sob, it's the other way round. It would kill me if Madoc went away.

'I'll call at seven,' he was saying, then, so softly it was like a whisper from the past, 'Wear the dress you wore for Morwenna's wedding.'

Over lunch, Morwenna said, 'I'm to take you shopping. I've had instructions from the big boss to help you choose a wedding outfit. So, no objections, now. See,' she opened her bag, 'I've got a blank cheque.'

'I'm not hard up,' Lynsey pointed out. 'I can afford something nice. It's going to be quiet. Didn't Madoc tell you?'

'Now I'll tell you something. Monique's been invited. You want to look better than her, don't you?'

Lynsey frowned, repeating, 'But it's going to be a quiet wedding, only close relatives.'

'My parents phoned her parents. They're insisting that Monique should come. I told you, she's almost part of the family, even without her involvement with—I mean,' she coloured, 'her friendship with Madoc. Are your parents coming?'

Lynsey shook her head and explained why not. 'David is, though, and Carole, his fiancée. Okay, so I'll get a *really* nice dress, but I'll pay——'

Morwenna shook her head. 'Boss's orders, I said, so come on.'

'Did my sister do as I instructed?' Madoc asked, as they waited for the meal to be served.

The restaurant was tucked away in a central London street, its ambience restrained and quietly opulent. It was bright with white tablecloths and colourful flower arrangements, while its menu bore prices which made Lynsey gasp but which Madoc ignored.

'She did. The dress is a pale cream, with long sleeves and—but you'll see it soon, won't you? Day after tomorrow.' She sighed. Everything was moving much too fast. She spread out her left hand. 'It cost an awful lot, like this ring must have done.' He had just given it to her. The sapphire gleamed in its setting of diamonds. 'Thank you for both.'

'I'm glad Morwenna insisted you used my cheque for the outfit.'

'Thanks for that. I'm not poverty-stricken, but I wouldn't have spent so much if I'd been paying. After all, it's going to be a very quiet affair, isn't it? I mean, you're making a big sacrifice, aren't you, giving up your freedom just because you slept with me and I was stupid enough not to take precautions?'

He didn't answer, not even after the waiter had gone, leaving them with their first course. So what did I expect him to do, she asked herself, deny it was a sacrifice to marry me, say he loved me madly?

In the silence that followed, she became conscious of the movement of his hands, seeing the strength in them, noticing the way the fine fit of his jacket gave emphasis to the broad shoulders; saw the rich darkness of his hair, the fine shape of his lips.

All these things she had seen that day she'd met him and she had loved them then. Love—it hadn't really been that, had it? She'd been infatuated with the man, with his aura of glamour, his self-possession, his faint aloofness mingling with the sensuality his eyes revealed.

He looked up and caught her eyes on him. She coloured deeply and said, 'Madoc, you're still a stranger. I don't know if what we're doing is right.'

He leaned back, one hand on the table, the other holding the glass of wine. 'You're questioning whether you and I should be marrying in two days' time?' He spoke coldly and objectively. Lynsey shivered inside. She had heard that voice in her ear when he had phoned her from head office. 'I think you'll agree that we have little choice in the matter.' He took a drink, watching her over the rim.

'Sorry,' she murmured, emptying her own glass too quickly down her throat.

'Unless . . .' He looked at her with eyes so hard they might have been chips of rock from the country in which he'd been born. 'Unless there is someone else, after all.'

'There's no one, Madoc, I swear there isn't. It's just that—well, I wish I *really* knew you.'

His eyes slitted to a cutting edge and Lynsey knew how he had made it to the top at such a relatively early age. His sister was right about his ruthlessness. Dig down a fraction, she thought, and you'd find granite reaching to the centre of his being.

'You wish you really knew me, hm?' His jaw moved, his eyes pinioned hers. 'I'd willingly oblige this evening, my sweet, but—we're just a little hampered at present, aren't we, in that respect?'

They stood in the centre of her living room and Lynsey looked up at him. His height, the breadth of his shoulders, his enormous self-confidence dwarfed the modest surroundings.

She reeled at the incredible truth that, the day after tomorrow, she would become this man's wife. He looked down at her, a half smile softening his mouth. If only, she thought, I had the courage to touch him.

As if he had read her thoughts—am I so transparent? she wondered—he took her hand and put it to his cheek, then repeated the action with the other. Her fingers tightened involuntarily, making indentations. His eyes, she saw, were dancing at their reversed roles, as if she were pursuing him.

'Well?' he said softly.

Lynsey shook her head, smiling. 'You're too tall for me, I'd have to stand on a footstool.'

His hands clamped around her waist and he lifted her so that her face was on a level with his. She gasped, waving her legs in the air behind her. 'No, no, I——'

He swung her so that her legs came forward, resting on his hips, and she found herself clinging to him for support. 'Now,' he said, waiting.

Her eyes, dazzled by the nearness of his face, closed tightly, then opened again. When she saw the character in its structure, the resolution in the chin and the firm set of the mouth, her heart reacted madly.

'I'm waiting,' he said, brown eyes glinting at her confusion.

Slowly, she closed the gap between her mouth and

his, tentatively brushing his lips, re-acquainting herself with the feel of them. They could, she thought dreamily, say such wonderful things, those lips, yet, at other times, tear a person to pieces.

'They're genuine,' he said with amusement, 'they're the real thing. Go on, taste them for yourself.'

She moved her head back, smiled widely at him, then, using her tongue tip, ran it along his lips and all the way back again.

'Who,' he said, his jaw hardening, 'has been giving you lessons in my absence?' He hoisted her across to the settee, lowering her to its shabby softness and joining her there.

His arms were soffocatingly tight. His eyes roved over her face, taking in each tiny detail, moving down to investigate the cleft which the low-plunging neckline revealed. She felt his thighs move against hers, giving them a spreading warmth.

'You've tormented me,' he said in almost an undertone, 'driven me crazy night after night.'

He can't, she thought, be talking about me. It must be Monique . . .

His mouth lowered, his resolute lips taking over, working on hers until they parted. Gaining access, the hard, seeking mouth took the softer, yielding one to itself, probing, exploring until its owner's head tipped back, drinking in every sensual movement the intruder made.

Lynsey's arms lifted, straining to maintain contact with the rigid, muscled body against which two male arms had roped her.

'Madoc,' she whispered, shivering as his mouth made its way to sensitive points around her neck, 'I've forgotten what it was like to be this close. We spent just a few hours together. We hardly know anything about each other . . .' Her fingers curled into his upper arms as the tip of his tongue sketched a tingling line around her ear.

'We're learning, and fast,' he muttered, running a hand over her body to rest on the piquant softness of her breasts. 'This dress,' he said, unfastening one by one the tiny buttons running from neckline to waist, 'its mix-up of colours, the way it follows every shape and curve—it's etched in my mind for good.'

'Or bad,' she countered, holding her breath at the stroke and play of his hand.

'Never bad. I'll always connect it with the glowing eyes of a girl on the stairs, shining out a message, saying, "I want you, come and get me".'

'I didn't,' she protested, yet knowing deep down that he was right. Seeing him, hadn't she immediately had the feeling, 'He's the one'? 'Yes, I did,' she admitted. 'I'd never been so attracted to a man before, just like that—at first sight.'

His head came up. 'Nor since?'

'No, no, nor since. After you, how could I feel that way about anyone else? Anyway, I've been so worried about whether I was——'

The telephone rang. 'Leave it,' Madoc muttered.

'No, no, it might be——' she slipped from under him, 'well, anybody.'

Into the telephone, she said. 'Lynsey here. Oh, it's you——' She slid her eyes sideways, opted for discretion and did not say the name.

'I've just heard,' Sam Wilkinson said, 'it came up the grapevine instead of down. Congratulations on your conquest.'

'Thanks, nice of you to——'

'I hope,' he broke in, 'Morgan appreciates his prize. He's a lucky man. Knowing his reputation,

I'd say you were wasted on him.'

'Sam, I——' How much could Madoc hear?

'I hope it doesn't mean we can't meet sometimes.'

'Sure we can meet—in the staff restaurant, lunchtimes.'

'I had in mind somewhere more private.'

The stillness behind her was unnerving. 'Th-thanks for phoning, Sam. 'Bye.' She turned, on the defensive, and annoyed with herself for being so. 'He sends his congratulations.'

'I heard.'

He must have heard the rest, in that case, she thought. 'He's—he's not a happy man at present. His wife's left him, taken their little son.' She rubbed her hands together nervously and gave a small smile. 'Strange how—how everyone tells me their troubles.'

He was standing now, tightening his tie, thrusting his hands into the pockets of his jacket. 'So there's been no one else?' His eyes had turned as cold as his voice. 'You were expecting him to phone. Don't shake your head. You said, "It could be——", then stopped.'

If I told him I'd meant David or even my parents, would he believe me? Definitely not, she decided. His passion had iced over and she wrapped her arms about her to keep herself warm.

'A car will call for you on Thursday. Eleven o'clock for eleven-fifteen.' He was at the door. 'Be ready.'

'Madoc——' Aren't we meeting before then? she wanted to ask, but his chilling expression froze the words in her throat. Instead, she offered, 'See you at our wedding, darling.'

His eyes flickered over her. He nodded and went away.

Now they were alone and driving a long way into the

bright afternoon. Lynsey reclined, eyes closed, in the passenger seat of Madoc's sleek, expensive car and let her mind drift back to the events which had led up to that moment.

On the dot of eleven, a large, dark limousine had called for her, its white ribbons fluttering. Someone had waited for her to answer the bell. For a long moment she had held back. All morning she had agonised—shall I ring Madoc, say, Call it it off, there's no need any more. My relief at your acceptance of the responsibility must have melted away that terrible tension I had, and . . .?

The ring had come again. Decision time was now, this minute, she'd told herself. *Whether it's right or wrong, I'm going through with it. I love Madoc, I want to be his wife. I'll face the consequences when they face me . . .*

'Dad!' she had exclaimed. 'Oh, it's so good to see you. But you're supposed to be away on business——'

'Postponed it,' he'd said gruffly, adding, 'You look lovely, my dear.' He stepped inside, smiling. 'Madoc, your intended, phoned us. He's a fine lad. As good as ordered us to present ourselves at the ceremony, said he'd fix the alteration of my appointment, knew my boss, no trouble. So here I am.'

'Mother, too?' Lynsey asked delightedly. Her father had nodded.

Would it be possible to talk to her, ask, What shall I do? But at the ceremony, there had been time only to meet her mother's brimming eyes, with not even a second to say, Please tell me if I'm doing right.

Then she had seen Madoc standing there and, in her heart of hearts, she knew that, loving him so much, she couldn't tell him her secret now.

Madoc, beside her in the bridal limousine, had worn

that unencouraging, slightly aloof air as they had
driven to the reception. When, for reassurance,
Lynsey had put her hand in his, he had turned to
smile, then withdrawn his eyes immediately to look
through the car windows.

Was he wishing, she wondered, that it was Monique
beside him? And what would he say if she were to tell
him, You could have had Monique as your wife after
all?

The driver had pulled up outside an imposing hotel
on the edge of the town. Cars were packed tightly in
the forecourt as though there were a company
conference in session.

'Madoc, why——?' she had started to ask. Why
such a place for a small, quiet wedding?

The hotel foyer was packed with people. David was
there, holding Carole's hand. A smiling woman said,
'Lynsey, my dear, welcome to the Morgan family.'

Lynsey recognised the face, one that had held
puzzlement and faint disapproval the last time she had
seen it—at Morwenna's wedding.

'Mrs Morgan, thank you,' she'd answered. 'But
please, tell me what's——'

'Here's the bride,' Mr Morgan exclaimed. 'Welcome, Mrs Morgan the second.'

'My dear.' Lynsey turned and almost fell into her
mother's arms. 'Every possible happiness, darling.
Your father and I can't say how delighted we are——'
She'd had to stop for tears.

'Oh, Mum, I——' But it was too late to ask
anyone's advice now. She looked around her. 'Mother,
tell me what's going on, *please*.'

'Nearly two hundred invited, dear,' her mother
whispered. 'Business acquaintances of Madoc's, your
father's bosses, uncles and aunts of yours and' she

smiled conspiratorially, 'the other side's. And Madoc wouldn't let us pay a single penny although we should have footed the bill.'

He turned at that moment.

'Why, Madoc?' Lynsey asked again as he led her through a doorway and into the room where they were to receive their guests.

One of Madoc's young cousins hurried along and freshened up the bridal bouquet, fixing it more securely in Lynsey's hands.

Madoc's smile reminded her momentarily of the Madoc she had first met. 'Don't you think you're worth it?' he'd asked.

For a few seconds, her heart had pounded with pleasure—he had done all this for her! No, said a whisper, not for you—for his position as a leading industrialist, head of a giant company that eats little companies like Lantern Scientific and tears them to pieces like a lion consuming its kill.

Handshakes, varying in pressure, came and went. Faces slid into focus, smiled, spoke a few words and moved away. There came another face, exquisitely structured, black hair dressed high, except where it cascaded over slender shoulders.

A hand came out, touching Lynsey's fingertips, only to be withdrawn as if it had touched barbed wire. The wide mouth was a pale, unsmiling line—until it moved by, quivered and opened to say, 'Madoc, darling.'

The reproach, Lynsey thought miserably, the pain which Monique had managed to infuse into those two words!

Two white, trembling hands found Madoc's, clinging convulsively, until he put them gently from him. Lynsey did not dare to steal a glance at his face.

If I saw in that the anguish I saw in hers, she thought, I'd want to crawl away and die.

'Crying, Lynsey?' The rhythm of the car had slowed and a finger sketched a tingling path around her throat.

'No, no, how could I be on my wedding day?' Lynsey wriggled up the seat and surreptitiously wiped the dampness from her cheeks. Should I tell him now, she thought—I married you under false pretences? Later, she told herself, later I'll tell him . . . 'Where are we going, Madoc?'

'Wales. Where else would I want us to go for our honeymoon?'

'Will the hotel be as grand as where we've just been?'

'What would your choice have been?'

'A cosy cottage for two, with a log fire for chilly weather and curtains billowing on sunny days.'

'You have a somewhat idealistic picture of life in the country,' he said smiling, then added, 'There are trees around it, flower beds, paths.'

There was an edge to his voice which stopped her from questioning him further. His profile was chiselled against the sky's deep blue. There seemed to be a subtle change in him. It was there in the supremely confident way he negotiated the curves and bends of the road, the narrowed concentration of his eyes as they dwelt on the hedgerows and the surrounding countryside.

Slowing the car, he signalled, turning across the road and moving through opened entrance gates and along a drive bordered with shrubs. In the distance mountains towered. Nearer was a line of low, green hills. A white, sprawling house came into view and Lynsey gasped.

'This place will cost a fortune, Madoc, even though we're only spending four days here.'

He did not comment, just drove slowly on.

Lynsey laughed uncertainly. 'How many stars does it have—five?'

'Fifteen, twenty, maybe,' he tossed at her, braking in front of the main entrance door and swinging out from the driving seat. 'I haven't counted lately.'

Something in the statement made her pause in the act of getting out. 'You've stayed at this hotel before, then?' He did not answer. 'With Monique, Madoc?' He held the car door, watching her straighten her jacket and skirt. 'Or—or maybe attending some conference or other?'

He opened the boot and pulled out their cases, standing back and motioning her into the house. Inside, she stared around, seeing the mushroom-tinted walls with high-reaching decorative panels picked out in white; the numerous doors opening off, the comfortable, tapestry-covered settees.

'Where are the other guests?' Lynsey asked, bemused. 'And where's reception? Madoc,' she smiled at him, 'is this a private country house and we're special guests?'

'It is a private house, my dear,' a woman came from an opened doorway, 'and you are indeed special guests. Madoc's wife,' she took Lynsey's hands, 'I'm so delighted to meet you. Madoc married at last—and what a pretty girl he chose!'

'Lynsey, my aunt Dilys, my mother's sister.'

Lynsey glanced from Madoc to the full-shaped, round-faced woman who looked at her with such pleasure. 'Madoc, why didn't you tell me?' she asked, 'I'd have been delighted to know we were going to spend our honeymoon at your aunt's house.'

'Oh no,' Dilys explained, 'not my place, dear. It belongs to Madoc. Where would I find the money to keep a mansion like this going?'

'This? All this is yours, Madoc?'

He nodded without expression.

'Madoc here,' his aunt went on, 'he's the one with the young fortune, aren't you, boy? And why haven't you told your lovely wife all about yourself? Madoc,' she drew him down by the shoulder and even then had to stand on tiptoe to kiss him on the cheek, 'how good to see you again. I live here, my dear,' she told Lynsey, 'I look after the place for Madoc, but any moment now,' she glanced at her watch, 'I'm off to stay with Rowena and her husband—my daughter's family.'

There was the sound of gravel crunching. 'There's the car for me now,' Dilys exclaimed. 'I've left food for you for the weekend. Look after her, Madoc. I'll see you both again very soon.'

A few minutes later, they were alone. 'All this,' Lynsey said, gesturing, 'all the way here, you could have told me, but you didn't.'

'A man could want to give his wife a pleasant surprise?'

The reproach went from her eyes. 'I'm sorry, Madoc. It's more than a pleasant surprise—it's just wonderful.'

'Glad you married me, now?'

This is the moment to tell him, she told herself. She took a breath to confess, but saw the ironic gleam in his eyes, with a tinge of anger mixed in. He was challenging her, she couldn't let that pass.

'Because of your wealth, you mean? Don't you know me better than that?'

'As you said yourself, our knowledge of each other

is almost nil. So the answer is no, I don't.' He looked her over, taking his time. 'For all I know, you might even have tricked me into this marriage.'

Lynsey paled, holding her throat and turning away. How could she defend herself now against such an accusation?

'Right at the start,' she said faintly, 'you said you wanted to marry me. I suppose that was just a spin-off from a couple of hours of passion?' She lifted her head, facing him. 'I pleased you for a while—even giving you the added kick of seducing a virgin, and it jogged your conscience, making you ask me to marry you!'

He caught her wrists and jerked her against him, eyes blazing. 'You were the one who ran away, thus terminating our association.'

'I did that *after* I knew who you were,' she defended herself, 'which answers your accusation that I married you for your money!'

He released her slowly. 'We both know why you married me, don't we?'

'You don't know, you don't!' she cried, turning away and covering her face. How had all this started? she wondered miserably. This was her wedding day— and she was crying . . .

CHAPTER FIVE

Two hands massaged her shoulders, turned her, pulled her against a hard, warm chest. 'Tell me why you married me, Lynsey.'

'Because I love you,' she answered in a muffled tone.

'As good a reason as any,' he teased softly, lifting her chin and placing his mouth on hers.

It was a waiting kind of kiss, she discovered. It didn't deepen. It stayed there, titillating the sensitive surface of her lips. Without warning, they came alive, tingling and quivering until she felt she couldn't stand it another minute.

On tiptoe, she reached up and pulled his shoulders down, pressing her mouth against his, even using her sharp, white teeth to provoke a response.

When it came, she had time only to gasp before she was enveloped in a hold so tight she thought her bones might break. Now it was his teeth nipping her flesh, making her squeal, the intrusion of his kiss turning her bones to water.

He let her go at last and she could only cling to him, cheek against him, hearing the thump of his heart and feeling the throb of her own.

'That's what happens,' he mouthed against her ear, 'when a wife tells her huband she loves him.' He eased her away. 'Time to show you round this mansion, as my aunt called it.'

Her eyes widened at each door he opened. There was the sitting room with sofas and chairs placed around a white, carved fireplace, low tables and tastefully placed lamps.

Then came the less formal living room, with its comfortable seating and boldly-draped windows, beyond which she could glimpse gardens and lawns and trees.

There was a dining room with shining furniture, a morning room for breakfast; the kitchen, whose proportions were surely designed for the large families of decades long past.

'And this,' Lynsey exclaimed, 'is just the ground floor! Can I see upstairs?'

'Like a small girl who's just been given a dolls' house,' he mocked as he led her upwards.

Lynsey lost count of the bedrooms, each one seeming to have its own bathroom or shower. The master bedroom was incorporated into a suite of three rooms, each leading out of the other.

One was a private living area, another a small office or study in the corner of which was a single bed tucked away. 'For use if we quarrel,' Madoc teased, leading her back into the main bedroom.

It was a large comfortable room, unpretentiously welcoming. The bed was large, its covers bright with a pattern which was echoed in the fabric of the floor-length curtains. A matching drape hung in soft folds from ceiling height, decorating the wall behind the bed.

'An idea of my aunt's,' Madoc said. 'She thought it would add a touch of softness to an otherwise—as she called it—very masculine room.'

'Would you object, Madoc, if I added some softer touches?' She touched his arm and he looked down at her hand.

'To the furnishings—or to me?'

'Both,' she answered smiling, 'certainly you. I have it on good authority, and going by my own observations—you're as hard as nails.'

He tugged at his tie, flipped open some shirt buttons and pushed her hand against his chest. 'Test now whether I'm hard.'

Loving the feel of him, she nodded. 'Like a stone wall.' She ran her fingertips over his rib cage, smiling at him provocatively. 'There's something behind it like an automatic pump.'

He looked down into her glowing eyes, then took her in his arms. 'It's a heart, lady. It may have a very tough outer shell, but inside, for you——' he crushed her mouth with his, 'for you, it's as soft as snow.'

Her head lay back on his arm. 'Snow's cold,' she said, smiling teasingly, 'snow can be packed into a hard, solid ball.'

'So melt me, Lynsey, give me some of your warmth.'

'Oh, Madoc, I——' Now, her common sense was shouting, tell him now.

'We share something, you and I, something we've created between us.' He moved slightly, placing a hand tenderly on her stomach. 'I'd make violent love to you this moment if I didn't have to treat you as if you were made of glass.'

A dagger of fear thrust into her somewhere near her heart. She must tell him the truth, tell him, there's no child coming, it must have been the terrible state of tension I was in, and the worry then the wedding preparations . . .

'Madoc, there's something I——'

'Hallo there, Mr Morgan?' A voice drifted up. 'It's only me, Gwyneth from the village.'

Madoc cursed softly but mildly, putting Lynsey from him and going on to the landing.

'Your aunt asked me to call in, Mr Morgan,' Gwyneth said, 'there's food to be cooked and she thought you and your wife wouldn't want to be bothered on your wedding day. I'll go away again, Mr Morgan, if you don't want me.'

He looked round, lifting his shoulders resignedly. 'Lynsey,' she joined him by the banisters, 'Gwyneth, who comes in to help my aunt. Gwyneth, my wife.'

'Hallo, Mrs Morgan,' said Gwyneth, 'very pleased to meet you. May I wish you both every happiness. Now, if you don't mind, I'll cook you some supper.'

In the bedroom, he pulled Lynsey close. 'My appetite needs something other than food to satisfy it, but,' he tweaked a curl, 'since that's out of bounds, we'll take a walk.'

Lynsey nodded, smoothing her hair. 'Shall we unpack later?' She glanced around the room. 'I still can't feel I fit in to all this. It's all happened so fast, I——'

'I can assure you, woman, you'll fit into me,' he said with a mocking smile, 'when I can touch you again.'

'Madoc, I don't now how to tell——'

'Sh-sh.' His finger went over her mouth. 'A walk, I said.' He took her hand and led her down the stairs, calling out to Gwyneth on the way.

They turned off the main gravelled path on to a lawn bordered by young trees. To the left was a winding path disappearing into woodland, while to the right the ground sloped away, leading to a paved area from which could be glimpsed a patch of liquid blue.

'A swimming pool?' Lynsey asked delightedly. 'If I'd known, I'd have brought a swimsuit——'

'Would that have been advisable in the circumstances?'

'What circum——?' Lynsey realised what he meant. 'Oh—oh, I—I suppose you're right.' How long, she thought, can I go on pretending? The more I delay telling him, the worse it will be. Later, she thought, not now but after dinner. You mean when he's mellow, that maddening voice asked, after food and wine?

Gwyneth served the meal in the dining room, having illuminated the room romantically with candles which glowed as the sky darkened. The paintings on the walls stared down, ancient portraits, country scenes, works which, Lynsey hazarded, if not priceless, were probably worth a great deal of money.

Did all those belong to Madoc, she wondered, not liking to ask in case he taunted her again with marrying him for his wealth.

She turned to him. 'Will you tell me something, Madoc? Will we always live in such splendour, so formally, I mean?'

He laughed, then pretended to whisper, 'Don't tell my wife, but all this has been laid on to impress her!' He added in a mocking voice, 'I can be extremely informal—when the time and the place and the circumstances are right all at the same time.' He laughed again as the colour crept into Lynsey's cheeks.

'In any case,' he went on, 'the time will come—in how many months?—when formality will go to the winds. When Morgan junior appears on the scene, hm?'

Was that really why he married me, she wondered sadly—to get himself a son? Probably—among all the other practical and impersonal reasons, that small voice reminded her.

That night, she stood uncertainly in the bedroom. Her cases had been unpacked, her clothes put away. Gwyneth had asked, 'Would you like me to?' and had done the work without waiting for an answer.

Where, Lynsey wondered, shall I undress? When she and Madoc had first made love, it had all been so easy, so unselfconscious. Passion, need, desire—they had all combined, fuelling the flames that had roared in their bodies, heating their emotions and making them forget themselves as individuals, bringing them together as one.

The whole situation was so different that Lynsey felt bewildered. Madoc's ring might be on her finger, but where was his passion now? He had stayed downstairs, probably giving her time to adjust. But I need him here, she thought, to help me do that—most of all, to come to terms with his presence in my life.

Taking a quick shower, she pulled on a silky robe—one which Morwenna had insisted she should buy—and searched for the matching nightgown.

'Can I help?' Madoc stood in the doorway, tall, lean, his features darkened by the subdued lighting shed from corners and curtained windows and bedside lamps.

His tie was gone, his shirt hanging loose and pulled free of his waistband. Even his hair was ruffled, as if he had run his fingers through it.

Lynsey straightened quickly, then remembered how much of her body showed through the peach-coloured négligée. Wrapping it round her more tightly only made things worse.

Madoc seemed amused by her confusion, strolling across and pulling free of his shirt. He moved her arms from around her, holding them wide and letting her robe fall open.

'I made love to you how many times that morning?' he asked. 'Yet I never once saw you looking so beautiful as you do now.' He ran his hand over her silky skin, down, down to her thighs and electrifyingly up again to hold a breast.

With a small, convulsive cry, she freed her arms and wrapped them round him, putting her face to the rough chest hairs and moving her lips against him.

'Madoc, oh Madoc,' she murmured, wanting reassurance and a statement of his love, thinking, how much longer will I be allowed to get near him, once he knows the truth?

'My sweet,' he groaned, enfolding her in his arms, 'if only I could make love to you right now, instead of having to hold myself back for the sake of the future generation . . .'

No, no, Lynsey thought, panicking now, he can't really be looking forward to having a child? He's only saying that to make me feel better at this moment about our reason for marrying—isn't he?

She lay in his arms, parting her lips to his, his arms cool and compelling on her heated flesh. It was all coming back—those feelings he had brought to life within her, the memory of his skin against hers, the sensation she had experienced of wanting to give every part of herself into his keeping.

There was no doubt at all, she acknowledged at last—she loved him, with all of her heart and soul she loved him.

'Love me,' she moaned, meaning, 'Tell me you love me, too,' but he misunderstood.

'My love, we must wait. Have patience for a few more weeks, until it's quite safe for lovemaking.' He moved her away and lifted her chin, smiling down. 'It would be terrible now, would it not, if the child was lost. After all,' he taunted softly, 'it was why we married, wasn't it?'

Unbelievably, he went to the door. 'If I slept beside you tonight,' he said, 'I wouldn't be able to hold myself back from making violent love to you. It's best if I use one of the other rooms. Don't you agree?'

Biting her lip to stop its trembling, she nodded.

'By heaven,' he said softly, 'if you keep looking at me like that, I'll take you here and now and to hell with what's to come.' Abruptly, he turned away, closing the door behind him.

Lynsey did her best to sleep, but the darkness weighed like lead on her eyelids. Lifting them, she was sure the room had grown smaller, the furniture almost threatening.

Reaching for the bedside lamp, she swung to the floor and pulled on the gown over her nightdress. The filmy fabric floated behind her as she wrenched open the door, glancing right and left in the dark corridor.

Which was Madoc's room? A door came open and he stood there, frowning. 'Can't you sleep?'

She ran to him, wrapping her arms around him and he pulled her into the room. It was large, but smaller than the master bedroom. A light glowed beside the bed, revealing a cover that was indented but otherwise undisturbed. He, too, had apparently found it difficult to settle.

He wore pyjama trousers, and Lynsey's cheek pressed against his ribs. 'There's something I have to tell you, Madoc,' she said, her voice muffled.

'That you love me, eh?' He was so indulgent, his voice so warm, she wanted to do anything but tell him the truth.

'It's true that I do,' she answered, 'but it's not that this time. It's——'

With extreme gentleness, he moved her slightly, looking down into her upturned face. 'Yes?' He spoke so tenderly, she could have cried.

It had to be said, it had been burning a hole in her dreams, turning them into nightmares.

'I'm not expecting a child, after all.'

CHAPTER SIX

SHE felt him go rigid. He pushed her arms away. There was a space between them now, a few paces that might have been a million miles.

'When did you know? Before the wedding?'

'Yes,' she whispered.

'So why did you go ahead and marry me?'

How could she say, 'It truly was because I love you'? She stayed silent.

'So I was tricked into this marriage after all.'

Lynsey winced at the bitterness, the acrimony in his tone. 'Madoc, that night at the hotel, when you came to my room, you proposed to me.' She could not help the waver in her voice.

'That,' he snarled, walking away, then turning to face her, 'as you said yourself, was just a spin-off from the lovemaking, as was your statement that you loved me.'

She shook her head, but knew it was useless to contradict. He would never believe now that it had been the truth.

'Are you,' she asked, 'accusing me of telling you I suspected there might be a child just to get you to marry me?'

'I am.'

'But I suspected there might be long before you asked me. I didn't come running to you begging you to marry me, did I? So where was the trickery in that? In fact, I'd decided that if I was pregnant, I would keep it to myself.'

'You changed your mind the moment I said I'd marry you, didn't you? Probably having calculated how much you'd gain financially from the marriage. So you played your cards right, deciding you'd keep up the pretence until you had my ring on your finger.'

'How can you think so badly of me?'

'By analysing every aspect of our discussions.'

He was talking, she thought, as if their relationship had been on a business footing and their marriage a convenient way of settling the problem!

'I honestly didn't want to trouble you.' His mouth twisted sceptically. 'At least give me the benefit of remembering,' she said bitterly, 'that I kept asking should we marry, because I wondered if we really knew each other well enough.'

'Of course you kept asking. To persuade me to disagree with the statement, to say we'd learn all in good time. After all, my motive for marrying you was strong—to protect, as I thought, the child I'd so carelessly produced.' His mouth twisted again. 'With your very willing help.'

Where she wondered, her heart aching, had all that feeling gone, the emotion they'd shared, the throb of excitement he had brought to her eager body, and the blaze of passion in his intense brown eyes? How contemptuously he was now dismissing the hours they'd spent together, a time she had come to regard as next door to paradise.

'Suppose I'd phoned you this morning and told you,' she asked, her eyes large with fatigue and dismay, 'what would you have done?'

'Cancelled everything.'

'Everything? The wedding, the reception—all those guests?'

'I'm a business man,' he answered, his jaw a rigid

line, 'and I'm callous. I lack compunction and feeling—your words—so why should I have worried about contacting the wedding guests and telling them, "Sorry, it's all off"?'

She stared at him, 'It wouldn't have been physically possible.'

'With the large staff I have at my disposal? Think again. I'd have compensated all those people very handsomely,' he said sarcastically, 'paid their fares and hotel bills, returned their presents. Oh yes, it would have been entirely possible. With sufficient cash in the bank, it's surprising what a man can do.'

'Even getting rid of a wife he doesn't want?'

'Even that.' He strolled towards her, his lean body taking on a strange menace in the half-light. 'But it's not something I have in mind at present.' He regarded her steadily, dwelling on her pale, serious face, her slender figure. 'Tell me something—why didn't you phone me the moment you knew there would be no child? After all, you assumed it would be a quiet wedding, one that would have been easily cancelled.'

How could she tell him, she wondered again, that she'd wanted to marry because she was so in love with him?

She stared up at him, eyes on fire. 'I was after your money and your social position, wasn't I? Why can't you accept that?' she cried, and raced back to her own room.

Dawn was a long time coming. Only then did she close her eyes and sleep. Waking heavy-eyed, she wondered where she was. Then it all came back and she rolled over, groaning.

How could her life have gone so disastrously wrong? If only—but people's lives were made up of those two sad little words. Well, she thought, sitting upright, I can't change the past, but surely I can do something about what's to come?

A glance in the mirror showed her two bright brown eyes and an oval face with a winsome expression. Hours of turning and twisting hadn't left as much of a mark as she had thought they might. But what did it matter how she looked?

I could, she told herself, look as beautiful as a beauty queen, but it still wouldn't make Madoc love me.

The smell of bacon cooking wafted upward as she made her way downstairs. Gwyneth, it seemed, had arrived already, which meant, Lynsey reasoned, that she and Madoc would at least have to be polite to each other in front of her.

Following the aroma, she found herself in the kitchen area.

'Breakfast's in the morning room, Mrs Morgan,' Gwyneth called from a room which opened out of the kitchen. 'If you'll just go in there,' she appeared at the inner door, 'and make yourself at home, I'll bring your breakfast. Are you choosy about what you eat, or——?'

'I'll have whatever's creating that lovely smell,' Lynsey told her, smiling back. 'I'm sure it'll be delicious!'

Gwyneth laughed and withdrew. The breakfast room had a cosy feel about it, the circular table being placed to one side and the fireplace piled with coals waiting for the first chill of autumn.

Madoc, Lynsey thought ruefully, would bring that chill in with him when he came, although it was the middle of summer. She took her seat at one of the set places and gazed at the sky through the window. It was a heart-warming blue, and tree branches stood out, green and rich, against it.

'That's Dan Evans, my boyfriend, cutting the grass,' Gwyneth said, hurrying in and motioning with her head towards a humming noise outside. 'Mr Morgan's given him a job. He was out of work, and it was eating into him. I told Mr Morgan and he said at once the two gardeners who work for him needed help.'

She placed a plate of steaming bacon and sausage in front of Lynsey. 'He's wonderful that way, is Mr Morgan. He was born here, you know,' she added proudly. 'Always helps whoever needs it if he possibly can.'

Gwyneth had finished unloading the tray of toast and coffee. 'Now get that into you, Mrs Morgan.' She took a look at Lynsey. 'Tired, are you? But then,' she grinned, 'I shouldn't ask that, should I?' She hurried away.

So it shows, Lynsey thought dismally; all those hours of lying awake and trying not to cry. At first she wondered how she could eat her breakfast, but her need for the food increased with the eating.

Putting her head round the door, Gwyneth enquired if anything further was needed Lynsey shook her head, asking, 'Has Mr—has my husband come down yet?' She nodded towards the other place setting.

Gwyneth looked at her a little curiously and Lynsey realised her mistake. 'Don't you know where he is, Mrs Morgan? Didn't he tell you?' She tutted. 'And on your first morning here. Said he was going for a dip, he did. A lovely pool it is, too. Thought he might have taken you with him!'

Outside, the sun played over Lynsey's bare arms, making her lift her face in gratitude. Its warmth soothed her tangled emotions, stroking away the shadows the night's restlessness had put beneath her eyes. What, oh what, she asked of all the plants and flowers around her, am I going to do now?

A man emerged through an opening in the hedge which surrounded the swimming pool. His hair was flat to his head and around his hips a towel was twisted, while another hung around his neck. A glance told him he was being watched. He made his way across the newly cut lawn, his lean body glistening in the sun's rays.

It's not fair, Lynsey thought. There he is, overflowing with life and energy, yet I'm limp as a dead flower. As each step brought him closer, her instinct was to make for cover rather than face him. It was only the thought of the sarcasm which would follow her that kept her still and braced for his disparaging glance.

A few paces away, he stopped, his eyes narrowing as they rested on her features. 'What happened?'

'I couldn't sleep for trying to think of a way out.'

'You could always run. The first time I saw you you were doing just that.' An ironic smile flickered over his lips. 'You seem to have been doing it ever since.' His hands went to his hips and, feet slightly apart, he stood in front of her. 'Why do you want a way out?'

'It's all such a mess, isn't it?' Her gesturing arm indicated the two of them. 'You married to me when it's obvious you don't want me. Me tied to you, when—when——'

'When you could so easily have married someone on your own level, who talked your own language and who told you incessantly that he loved you. Is that right?' His eyes were diamond-bright, his mouth an unforgiving line.

She had been going to say, when it's quite obvious you'd rather be free of me now there's no child coming, but all she said was, 'Think what you like.'

He took the towel from around his neck and rubbed his chest in a circular motion, looking her over thoughtfully. 'There's a way round our dilemma.' He went on rubbing until the dark hairs curled thickly and his flesh glowed.

Lynsey had to look away to control an urge to press herself to him, holding on to the sinewy muscle of his upper arms and whispering her love.

He smiled. Had he read her mind? He held out the towel. 'My legs are damp. Rub them, will you?'

Lynsey went pink and gazed back at the house. 'Madoc, people will see us . . .'

'Just Gwyneth. Give her something to talk about when she gets home. All the village will be wanting to know how Madoc Morgan and his bride were behaving themselves on their honeymoon. They'll be disappointed about one thing—that we didn't stay in bed all day.'

He thrust the towel at her and she took it shyly, crouching down and rubbing slowly at the hard columns of his legs. She looked up and found his arms were folded and there was a self-satisfied smirk on his face.

She flung the towel down and made for a clump of distant trees. In a moment, he was on her heels, tripping her up and catching her as she fell, pulling her down on top of him in the shadow of some bushes.

His towel had loosened and she felt his hard arousal. 'No, no, Madoc,' she said.

He twisted her under him and smiled broadly into her frowning face. 'No, Madoc—what? Good grief, woman, it's our honeymoon. Aren't I even allowed a kiss?' And his mouth hit hers, working at her lips and forcing an entry, taking the taste of her into him as if he were savouring a vintage wine.

Then he stilled and raised his head, moving from her and rearranging the towel. 'We have to talk.' He pushed her skirt aside and ran a reflective finger along her inner thigh. Immediately, her body began to respond to him. He saw it, she was sure, but he did not follow it up. 'I'll take you sightseeing. We can discuss our future then. There's an answer to our problem.'

Bewildered, she looked at him as he lay still beside her. He had turned on the passion, then turned it off as if he had operated a piece of machinery. Had he used it the day they had met, flicking on a love-switch, then, when he was done, switching it off again?

Hills rose all around, tree-capped and green, as they drove towards Snowdonia. Dark greens changed to light when the sun slid from behind a cloud, flooding the landscape. On the valley floor were fields and drystone walls.

The road took them towards the mountains massed in the distance and, before long, they were among them. On each side the summits and rock faces rose dauntingly.

'Just look up there,' Lynsey exclaimed, seeing moving dots of red, yellow and blue.

Madoc slowed the car. 'Climbers. They're a fairly common sight in these parts.'

'I'm sure they'll fall! It's like a solid wall of rock.'

Madoc laughed. 'Can't you see the ropes? They're quite at home, probably climbed these peaks many times before. That's Glyder Fawr they're tackling, over three thousand feet.'

Great boulders lay tumbled haphazardly down the mountain's slopes, while rough-edged rocks lifted out of the sparse layer of greenery and grassy tufts.

'There's Snowdon,' said Madoc, pointing to a particularly high range of mountains. 'A train climbs all the way to the summit. I'll take you on it one day.'

It was a promise that sounded so precious, Lynsey wanted to cup it and hold it like a rare butterfly. 'One day' implied that there might be a future to their relationship. But people made promises like that to children to keep them quiet, didn't they?

Precipices rose right and left, paths criss-crossed the lower hillsides, spectacular summits loomed into the far distance while, at each turn and curve of the road, fresh mountain ranges swung into view.

Madoc pulled into a parking bay and gestured to a rough track which led away down towards a distant lake. 'That's where we're going. There's a packed lunch in the back, courtesy of Gwyneth.' He stretched an arm along the seat so that her head rested on it. 'All right by you?'

'More than all right,' she answered, unable to banish the happiness from her eyes.

Why can't it always be like this between us? she wondered and got out of the car as a gull swooped past.

They dropped half-way down a hill overlooking a cluster of cottages and farms. In the near distance was a lake, surrounded by mountains and catching the sun's glint as it emerged from cloud cover.

Wherever the eyes came to rest, there were slopes and sun-splashed hills and Lynsey hugged herself at the beauty of it all mingling with the joy of being with the man she loved.

He lifted the picnic basket to her side. 'You be

mother,' he quipped and, narrow-eyed, watched her wince. His implacable expression told her he had not used the phrase unthinkingly.

'There's one thing you won't be,' she retorted, needing to hurt him back, 'and that's a father.' Something inside had made her retaliate but, when she saw his jaw jerk angrily, she regretted her impetuous statement.

After the food had been packed away, Madoc lay back, arm behind his head, his long legs outstretched. Lynsey hugged her knees and gazed at the dark side of the hill across the valley.

'I suppose,' she commented, 'you know every inch of this terrain.'

'I should, shouldn't I? It was in these parts I was born and bred.' The lilt in his voice caught at her heart.

'Gwyneth told me. She also said,' she stole a glance at him and found with a faint shock that his eyes weren't closed, but were staring unreadably at the cloud formations above them, 'that you help anyone who needs it if you possibly can.' She reached out and picked up a pebble, running her thumb over its smooth surface.

'Did that bit of information improve your opinion of my terrible character?'

'I never doubted that you were honourable. That night you—we—made love, you gave me the choice.'

'Glad you realise that.'

'Also, you did offer me marriage to cover any— eventuality.'

He smiled and saluted mockingly.

'But that was on a personal level. I can't judge yet, can I, whether your business integrity is good or bad, except by hearsay.'

'And hearsay's something you do listen to,' he derided, 'hence your mad scamper like a frightened rabbit from a fox after hearing at Morwenna's wedding who I was.'

'There's a saying, "No smoke without fire". People say,' she went on before he could retaliate, 'that you lay about you with a scythe among the employees when you take over a company. There was the case of David's friend, Neville Blackmore, who had a wife and family. You sacked him——'

He frowned. 'Blackmore? He took a job we offered him in Scotland, at one of our subsidiaries. How much of a friend is he to your brother?'

'I've lost touch with him,' David had said. 'Oh,' Lynsey said, astonished at the information. 'I'm very glad to hear that. But there was that woman secretary with an invalid husband. Her boss left, so you——'

'Sacked her? Correction. She turned down every alternative position we offered her. So she resigned. Wanted somewhere nearer her home, she decided.' His eyebrow lifted sardonically. 'Any more false rumours for me to correct? So how about an apology for your accusations?'

Lynsey glanced at him under her lashes. 'Sorry again, although I'm very pleased to hear the truth. But,' her look challenged him this time, 'there's another rumour.' She saw the grim line of his mouth, but something drove her on. 'It's going round that you're going to eliminate the research department at Lantern Scientific.'

'Go on,' he said, his voice hard. He was frowning at the clouds now. Lynsey was glad that his black gaze was not on her.

'Is it true, that rumour, Madoc? You see,' she ignored her better judgment and went on, 'they're all worried. Des, my brother David and his fiancée, Carole. Those two want to get married, but they couldn't if they lost their jobs.'

He sat up and she felt herself sway away from him instinctively. 'What are you after now,' he said in a dangerously quiet voice, 'a little bit of nepotism on my part?'

'No, no, the idea never occurred to me!' She hurled the pebble away.

He ignored her shocked response. He reached out and jerked her face round. 'Using your position already, are you? Been married to me for a day and you're putting pressure on me to give preferential treatment to your relations!'

She tried to scramble free but he twisted on to his knees and pulled her up to face him. He held her shoulders, his lips covered hers and the pressure he used to gain entry to her mouth pushed her backwards, putting a strain on her knees and back that made her whimper with pain.

Then he eased her forward, pulling her round and on to her back beneath him.

'You hurt me,' she accused, 'how could you! But it's part of you, isn't it, it goes with your character— oh . . .'

He cut off her words with his kiss, rubbing his tongue against her teeth, then exploring her inner lips until she surrendered her mouth to him. His hand penetrated the fastenings of her dress, making her breast throb with caresses and she found herself cupping his head and pressing it down as if she never wanted him to let her go.

When he did, he lay back and rolled her against his side. 'And that,' he said at last, 'is the answer to our dilemma.'

'What is, Madoc?' she asked dreamily, happy just to be close to him after his outburst of passionate anger.

'To make no pretence of loving but to be honest and admit that we enjoy each other; to live under the same roof but making no demands emotionally.'

'Only physically?'

'Sexually.' He ran his hand over her body. 'Don't be afraid of using the word.'

The whole idea filled her with dread but, she tried to reason, if that was the only way in which she could stay close to the man she loved, then she would accept it, and gladly.

In the early afternoon they returned, Madoc swinging the car to brake in front of the house.

He took Lynsey's hand on to his knee. 'You accept my solution to our problem, hm?' He curled her fingers and brushed her knuckles against his lips.

'Cohabitation without emotion?' She smiled at him provocatively.

'Precisely.' He lowered his eyes to dwell on her dishevelled hair and clothes. 'I provide you with all the worldly goods you could possibly want, while you provide me with——'

'Sexual fulfilment.' She snatched her hand away. The idea angered her but, she told herself again, the alternative is—what? An empty life, because any life without Madoc would be empty.

'Well?' His eyebrows lifted. He was waiting like a man expecting a prospective employee's acceptance of the proffered conditions of service.

'Yes,' she answered, 'but——'

'But what?'

'It goes against the grain,' she said and ran from the car.

After washing and changing into a sleeveless dress of printed silk, Lynsey lay on the large bed and wondered how, with her warm nature, she could live side by side with Madoc and yet not show her feelings for him. But what, she asked herself yet again, was the alternative?

Sighing, she told herself once more just what that was. Separation for the length of time required by law, followed by the pain of divorce, readjustment, picking up the pieces of her life and fitting them together again—and finding there was one vital piece missing.

She rolled on to her side. Why had her life become so packed with problems? It had been so straight-forward, so uncomplicated before that fateful day she had met Madoc Morgan . . .

Her own soft breathing awakened her, probably because she was so unaccustomed to sleeping at that time of day. Startled, she discovered it was evening.

Wondering where Madoc had gone, she smoothed her dress and combed her hair so that it curled softly around her face. Had Madoc tried to find her? The sound of a car drawing up outside took her to the window, but she was too late to see who the visitor was.

A fair-haired young man worked on a flower bed edging the drive. Nearby, a few feet from him, an old blue van was parked, its rear doors open.

Gwyneth appeared and walked across to the man, rubbing her hands on her apron. It must, Lynsey assumed, be Dan, her boyfriend. They exchanged a few words and looked speculatively at the small white car which stood in front of the main entrance. Gwyneth shook her head and glanced upward to the windows where Lynsey stood.

At once, Lynsey moved out of sight but not before

she saw Gwyneth's frown. Maybe, Lynsey thought, it's because I'm late for evening drinks, since it was surely too early for dinner to be served?

Someone was talking. The voice was high-pitched and persuasive. A woman's voice, it drifted up to Lynsey as she descended the stairs. It's probably Madoc's Aunt Dilys, Lynsey hazarded a guess. She must have returned unexpectedly.

'But why did you marry her?' the voice asked as Lynsey reached the living room door. 'I was here, darling, you could have had me any time, with or without a ring. You know how it was in the old days—you and I. It could have been like that again . . .'

There were sobs and choked words. 'I love you, you know that. You told me you wanted a wife who fitted in with your work-load and lifestyle. Well, I'd have given up acting like a shot to be with you wherever you had to go, even your trips abroad.'

There were more sobs, tearing at the speaker's throat. Was this, Lynsey thought bitterly, the woman's greatest bit of acting in her career to date?

'Hush, Monique,' Madoc's voice was warm, caressing. 'All right, so our families expected an engagement, but never once did I suspect that you——'

'I was waiting for you to ask me, that's all,' Monique sobbed, 'to ask me to marry you. Instead, you asked *her* . . .'

The door moved from Lynsey's grasp, swinging noiselessly open, sufficient for her to catch a glimpse of disordered, luxurious dark hair running through Madoc's fingers, a flushed and beautiful face upraised, lips parted to receive his lingering kiss.

Treading like a cat, Lynsey streaked upstairs, threw an armful of personal belongings and clothes into a case and tiptoed down again. If he wanted Monique, she thought, anger and despair burning her up, then he could have her. But shouldn't I have known? she questioned silently. Hadn't he warned her that, as far as he was concerned, Monique would always be around?

'Listen to me, honey,' Madoc was saying, 'I married her because I——'

'Honey,' he'd called her! When, Lynsey thought, moving out of earshot, has he ever addressed a single word of endearment to me?

She tore along the hall, pushing into the kitchen and looking distractedly for Gwyneth.

'*Noswaith dda*, Mrs Morgan,' Gwyneth said, appearing at the inner door. 'Good evening, can I get you anything?' Then she saw the pain in Lynsey's face, added to it the bulging suitcase and exclaimed, 'Whatever's wrong?'

Lynsey shook her head, trying to control her voice. She gestured behind her, took a breath to speak but pressed her lips together.

'It's that Miss Merion, isn't it?' Gwyneth asked, voice full of sympathy. 'I said to Dan just now that woman's come to make trouble. It's married to him she wants to be, but she can't have him now.'

'She—she can have him,' Lynsey got out. 'He—he doesn't want me, Gwyneth. Never did ... I can't tell you, not now. But——' She wiped her cheek with her wrist as it held her handbag, and peered outside. 'That's Dan out there, isn't it? Well, could he give me a lift, please?' She put down her case and mopped up the tears. 'To the nearest railway station would be fine.'

'But Mrs Morgan, you're not leaving your husband? Not on your honeymoon?'

'He's got to decide which of us he wants. If it's me,

Gwyneth, he'll know where to find me. If it's her ...'
She steadied her voice and lifted her shoulders.
'That's it, isn't it? So please, ask Dan, will you?'

Peering from the window of the small blue van, she
saw Gwyneth's sadly shaking head.

'Please don't tell anyone about this, Gwyneth, will
you? Not your family, nor anyone. Not yet, not until I
know which of us he ...' She couldn't go on.

'What shall I tell Madoc Morgan if he asks me
where you've gone?' The van began to move.

'That it takes two, not three, to make a marriage
work,' Lynsey called through the window and turned
her face resolutely from Madoc's beautiful white
mansion.

CHAPTER SEVEN

LYNSEY was never more glad than now that she had
not given up her little flat. There had been so little
time between Madoc's agreement to marry her and the
ceremony itself that she hadn't even notified the
landlord that she would be quitting.

The day crept by and Lynsey's ears grew tired of
the silence. They had been listening unceasingly for
the sound of the telephone, even inventing a ring
inside themselves to compensate for the absence of the
real thing.

Monday morning, she thought, and now it's back to
normality—except that she knew things would never
be the same again. After all, hadn't her name changed,
for a start?

Lynsey Morgan ... She played with the sound,
saying the words aloud, then felt like weeping because
it was all a charade. She was no more Madoc Morgan's
wife now, except for a piece of paper, than she had
been before she met him.

'David,' she saw her brother as she entered the
laboratory in which he worked, 'could you spare a few
minutes?'

'Sure.' He smiled, then frowned. 'What went wrong
on the honeymoon, then?'

'You've guessed? Oh, David ...' She turned away,
putting a hand to her face. Brother-like, he waited,
making no move to comfort her, but she felt his
sympathy instinctively. 'I've left him, David. He—he
doesn't love me, never did. You know that. And you

know why we married. Well, that reason's gone now.'

'No kid?'

Lynsey shook her head. 'It built up in my mind, the image of a baby.' For the first time, she allowed herself to acknowledge just how disappointed she had been after discovering a child had not even begun to exist—Madoc's child and hers.

'No time like the present,' David commented. 'It'd all be legal and cosy, with a married mum and dad to call its own.'

Lynsey had to smile, but she shook her head. 'He's got the woman he really wants now. Her name's Monique Merion, daughter of friends of the family. They were all expecting him to marry her, anyway.'

David frowned. 'Haven't I heard of her—film actress, up and coming?'

'Film or stage, I don't know which. Well, aren't you going to tell me I'm a fool to have left him and that I didn't give our marriage a chance?'

'You're old enough now to know what you're doing.' He smiled, an older brother smile. 'You always did make yourself scarce, even as a kid, when things started to go wrong. Ran like a scared rabbit and went into your burrow until life straightened itself out.'

'Self-preservation instinct, pure and simple. So you don't blame me? Thanks for that.'

'The parents won't like it. Okay,' he patted her hair, 'I won't be the one to tell them. That's your prerogative. Keep it between ourselves for as long as you want.'

All day, Lynsey expected a call from the chairman's secretary, a furious message to *Miss Thorpe* to come to his office at once. It didn't happen and it began to register on Lynsey's mind that it really was all over between them.

If he'd really wanted me back, she told herself, he would have phoned me on Friday night after I'd got home. He would have rung and rung until I answered. Even if he'd sworn at me, he would at least have demonstrated that he wanted me in his life again . . .

As she left the office on her way home, a man turned the corner and she almost bumped into him. Her heart, having leapt, subsided when she saw who it was. I'm seeing Madoc in everybody, she thought, concerned at her reaction. If I feel like this about him, how many years is it going to take me to adjust to his absence from my life?

'Lynsey,' Sam Wilkinson exclaimed, 'how are things with you?'

It seemed light years since she had seen him, heard his problems, tried to give him advice. Now, she thought with bitter irony, I need a sympathetic ear to pour my troubles into.

'Not too bad,' was her unthinking reply, and saw his puzzled response.

'That's lukewarm for a bride of how many days? Four?'

She lifted her shoulders and there must have been something in her face that stopped him from questioning her further.

'You?' she asked.

He made a face and shook his head. 'I still don't know where my wife is, but I've had a letter from her, via her solicitor. She tells me she's not returning our son under any circumstances.'

His plight touched her. 'Sorry to hear that, Sam.'

'Look,' his hand detained her, 'I know you're married now, but—could we meet some time, have a chat, a drink, together? I get lonely,' he explained, 'and a bit morbid, sitting at home, thinking about where I went wrong in my marriage.'

That makes two of us, she thought sadly, nodding and saying, 'A coffee, some time, Sam? See you around, then.'

'Going home? I'll walk with you to the car park.'

Together they went down the stairs to the main entrance. 'Did you enjoy your honeymoon?' Sam asked as they made their way through rows of parked cars.

'It was fine,' she answered, hoping she sounded convincing.

'I imagine it'll take you some time to adjust to your new environment?'

'Yes, it will,' she answered automatically, 'but——' The rest of the answer stayed in her throat. Across the car park a man was locking a large, green car. He was tall, with a long, strong physique and eyes as powerful and penetrating as laser beams. They were on her now, those eyes. They were piercing a hole in the centre of her heart.

'Got your keys?' Sam asked, wondering at her hesitation. 'Give me them, I'll unlock for you. You seem,' he smiled, 'to be in a bit of a dream. Not surprising, I suppose,' he said with more than a trace of bitterness, 'with only a few days of marriage behind you.'

He stood back and put himself right in the path of those eyes. Were they burning him, too? Quickly, Lynsey slid into the driving seat, lifted her hand and drove off, thankful that the way out did not lead past the man with the large green car.

Morwenna phoned that evening. 'Lynsey,' she exclaimed, 'tell me what in heaven's name is going on between you and my brother.'

'How did you know I was here?' Lynsey asked, giving herself time to think of an answer.

'I rang Madoc at his home and said I wanted to speak to you. You weren't there, he said. He didn't know where you were but, he said, knowing you as he was coming to know you, you'd probably scampered back to your mousehole. He sounded furious, Lynsey. I've never known him so angry. Just tell me—*why?*'

'Lots of reasons, Morwenna. I'll tell you some time. It wouldn't have worked. In fact, it was already going wrong. I heard him talking to Monique. She came to the house——'

'Wrapped herself round him, did she?'

'He fell for it, Morwenna.' Her voice faltered. 'You told me yourself that everyone expected them to marry.'

'But they didn't, did they? He married you. So——?'

'All right, I'll tell you why. We made love,' she blurted out, 'after your wedding, Madoc and I. He thought there might be a child . . . so did I. He proposed—it was the honourable thing to do, he said. Also, he probably thought,' with a deep bitterness, 'that I might tell the world and smear his name in the eyes of his colleagues, not to mention the business world in which he's so highly regarded.'

'Oh dear,' said Morwenna. 'But couldn't you have given the marriage a chance?'

'With his lady friend crying out to him from the sidelines? And him reassuring her and saying it's okay, she's just my wife—you're the woman I really love. You see, he told me Monique would always be there, whether he married me or not. Do you understand now?' There was no answer. 'Morwenna, don't you see? He was as good as telling me that although I might become his wife, he reserved the right to keep Monique as his mistress.'

'Maybe I do see,' Monwenna answered slowly, 'now you've explained.'

'He hasn't even tried to contact me since I left him in Wales last Friday. If he really wanted me back, don't you think he'd at least have rung to ask if I'd got home safely?'

'Every man has his pride,' Morwenna pointed out. 'Not that I'm trying to excuse him. If I'd run out on Griff and he hadn't come after me to get me back, I'd have been furious, I must admit. Well, keep in touch,' she finished airily, secure in the knowledge that her own marriage was based on love.

Having little appetite for an evening meal, Lynsey took a tray into the living room and ate cheese rolls and an apple while watching television. It was a comedy show and her eyes followed the actors' movements, but her laughter mechanism, which was usually so responsive, had gone completely out of action.

She took the tray into the tiny kitchen, then froze as the doorbell rang. Speaking into the entryphone, she said, 'Sam?' It couldn't have been anyone else. She just couldn't listen to his problems now, not until she'd solved her own. She started to open the door.

'I'm so sorry, but I'm——' Her hand went to her mouth. Sam knew she was married and would have assumed she no longer lived at that address. Too late to replace the door chain; the visitor was over the threshold and fastening the door behind him.

'You're sorry but you're—what?' Madoc clipped, eyes ravaging her. 'Not dressed up enough to let him in—or perhaps I should have said *dressed down*?' He lifted himself from the door. 'I'd have thought you'd have brought him back with you, but then I was there, wasn't I, watching you in the car park? What did you whisper as you got into the car—"tonight, seven-thirty"?'

'I'm sorry, Madoc, but you can't come in. It's over between us. I've left you——'

He brushed her aside and went across to the television set, switching it off. He turned, brushing back his hair with both hands, straightening his shoulders as if all day the weight of his responsibilities had made them ache.

His suit was, as ever, impeccably cut, the faint red stripe of his shirt matching the dark red of his tie. This he started to remove, his eyes holding hers, mocking the surprise in them and the growing realisation of his intention.

'You can't stay.'

He glanced at the clock on the mantel-shelf. 'When he comes, let him in. I'm easy. Our marriage doesn't preclude an affair or two on the side——' his drawl changed into a snarl, 'provided it's well away from your—and the company's—own doorstep. Provided your lover doesn't come skulking around when I want your services.'

Lynsey's face flamed at the insult. 'It's over, do you hear? Will you get out?'

He did not move, just rested his hands against his lower back, letting his jacket drape over them.

'You don't want me around any more,' she declared. 'You can even have these back.' She tugged at the rings, but they would not move. Her voice rose in frustration. 'The whole reason for our marrying is null and void now, you know that.'

His smile did not touch his eyes. 'Too bad you married me, then. You knew the score when you decided to go through with the ceremony even when it became apparent that my offer of an honourable marriage no longer applied.'

She stared at him. His jacket was following his tie to a chair. He was seating himself on the couch, leaning back, resting his head on his upraised arms.

'If you offered me a drink, I wouldn't say no.'

'The sort of drink I keep here would offend your fastidious palate.'

'Try me.' His smile taunted and he stretched lazily, the muscled lines of his body making Lynsey's heart miss a beat.

She swung away, going to the sideboard and lifting out a bottle. It bore the name of a famous chain of supermarkets. Pouring the liquid into a glass, she thrust it at him. 'Now sneer at that.'

He lifted it to the light, raised his eyebrows appreciatively at the colour, then put it to his lips and drank. 'I've tasted a lot worse coming out of "famous name" bottles.' He tipped the rest down his throat and held out the glass. 'I'd like a refill, thanks. Join me with one of your own.'

She wanted desperately to refuse, resenting his autocratic tone, but knew he would laugh if she did. Holding her glass, she turned on the television on the way back to the couch, hesitated between joining Madoc on it and an upright chair, finally choosing the seat beside him for the same reason as she had poured herself a drink.

He had watched her vacillating manoeuvres with sleepy eyes like a lion who knew he had a mouse at his mercy. He glanced at the clock. 'When's he coming? Five minutes? Thirty? Is that why you're so jumpy?'

You're twisting my nervous system into knots, she wanted to shout, that's why I'm jumpy. 'If by "he" you mean Sam Wilkinson, he's not coming. I was going to have a quiet evening, if you must know.'

An empty evening, she thought, a desert of an evening . . . And now you've come here and turned it into a jungle from which I can't find a way out.

He took a drink, his eyes still on her. 'I like your outfit.'

'This?' She looked down at herself, seeing the old pink top she had pulled on, its neckline curved low, having stretched with wear and washing, the rest of it perversely having tightened up. Her trousers were ancient, too, out of fashion and hugging her figure. 'I've had these years. Which proves, doesn't it, I wasn't expecting anybody?'

'Don't fall over yourself trying to explain how innocent your life is after deserting the man you married.' He took her empty glass and put it beside his. 'I saw you with the man you've run to. I saw you with him at the barbecue.'

'So what does that prove?' she asked shrilly. He was getting under her skin. 'I told you, his wife's left him——'

'Snap,' he interposed dryly. 'And you're all set to take her place.'

'Look Madoc——' She paused, denial was useless. 'Why did you come here?'

'To see my wife.' He unfastened a couple of buttons on his shirt. 'To refresh my memory of how she looks when she smiles——'

'I'm not smiling,' she snapped, immediately regretting the childish response.

'Of how she looks,' he went on, eyes sliding over her broodingly, 'when she's naked. It's been a long time,' he reached out and seized her arm, pulling her sideways, 'since that first time.'

Panic gave her extra strength and she twisted free,

hurting herself as she did so, rubbing her arm and looking down at him.

'I want you to go.' He did not move. All the time the figures flitted across the television screen, the volume turned low so that the words could hardly be heard. She repeated, more loudly. 'I want you to go, Madoc.'

He saw a tabloid newspaper lying on the floor, picked it up and scanned its pages.

Lynsey gritted her teeth. 'Will you get out!' Panic was treading on her heart, accelerating it to racing-car pace. She reached out and jerked his shoulder, desperate to remove him.

His face was wiped clean of tolerance. He threw the printed pages aside, caught her waistband in clawing fingers and swung her down and on to the couch. He flung her backwards and forced her wrists high above her head.

'I've taken one hell of a lot from you,' he said between his teeth. 'I behaved towards you with honour, only to have my honourable gesture thrown back in my face. You as good as admitted you'd tricked me into marrying you——'

'Oh no, Madoc, believe me, I didn't!'

He jerked her hands even farther from her body, ignoring her whimper. 'Why the hell should I believe a word you say? You told me you accepted my solution to our problem, then took to your heels the moment my back was turned.'

Her eyes were watering with the pain he was inflicting, both physically and on her emotions. 'I left you because you were as good as making love to the woman you really wanted. She was sucking up to you and you were receiving her with open arms. You can't deny it. You don't love me, you love her. Admit it!'

'I admit nothing,' he said though his teeth. 'Except one thing. I want you, body and soul I want you. Which, my love,' he snarled, 'is why I'm here. Which answers your question, doesn't it?'

'No, no, you can't, you mustn't ...' She squirmed beneath his bruising hold.

'There's no physical barrier between us? Tell me, is there?'

He was being considerate again and she could hardly bear it. This was the side of him she loved, the side he had shown her when they had first met, the side she could scarcely resist.

'None,' she whispered.

He nodded and released her, leaving her limp with anti-climax and, she had to admit it, disappointment. His smile told her he knew it and was taking a malicious pleasure from it. He retrieved the newspaper and leaned back, reading it, appearing to have dismissed her from his mind.

Tugging at her rumpled top, she dropped back to the couch and, unseeingly, watched the television screen. Her mind was asking, what shall I do with him? When will he go?

After a while, he lowered the paper, folding it. 'What's it about?' he asked, indicating the screen.

'I don't know,' she answered, then could have kicked herself.

He smiled broadly at her give-away reply and got up, wandering around, glancing into the kitchen, finding the bedroom but making no comment.

'You won't mind, then, if I turn this off.' He did so and continued wandering. 'Don't you like music?'

'I love it,' she answered indignantly.

'Where's the hi-fi?'

'It's a luxury I haven't been able to afford. Oh, I

could have bought second-best, but it would offend my ear.' She touched it. 'It's very sensitive.'

'I'll remember that.' He smiled at her annoyance. He pushed his hands into his pockets, tautening the fabric, revealing the wide strength of his hips, then watched with amusement as Lynsey had to tear her eyes away. 'You should come to my place some time,' he said, eyelids drooping, assessing the swell of her breasts, 'and listen to mine. It's first-class, the best money can buy.'

It was an invitation with sensual overtones that had the colour sweeping into her cheeks. It had also been deliberately phrased, she was sure, to let her know just how much she was missing by deserting him as she had.

'W-what place?' she asked.

'My London flat.' He rocked on his heels, slanting a glance down at her, as if he were sizing up her potential for a night's seduction in his bed.

'I—I didn't know you had a——'

'London flat? You never asked so I never told you. No point now, is there?' He was taunting her like someone holding a tasty morsel out of a kitten's reach.

'No,' she said boldly, and wrenched herself to her feet to escape the terrible sense of loss which was weaving itself in and out of her emotions. 'I want to go to bed now, Madoc. I'm tired. So,' her arm indicated the entrance lobby, 'do you mind?'

'Not at all,' he answered blandly and dropped to the couch. 'Carry on. I'll let myself out when I'm ready.'

'You can't stay!' she cried. 'I'll have you put out. I—I'll call a neighbour.'

'Go ahead. He folded his arms, crossed his legs, looking as permanent as a Welsh mountain. 'I'll tell them I'm your husband.'

'Oh!' She swung away and slammed her bedroom door. Undressing quickly, she pulled on a dressing-gown and emerged, flushed and angry, making for the bathroom. She stopped dead. The living room was empty. Madoc had gone.

She lay on her back, tense and unhappy, having washed and got ready for bed at record speed. Asking herself why, she had to admit she didn't know. Madoc wouldn't come back, not now, not ever.

She had made it plain to him, hadn't she, that everything between them was over? All right, so he had said he wanted her, but that had been just to annoy her.

Sleep must have come quickly, although she had been sure it wouldn't. She awoke with a start and found with astonishment that barely half an hour had passed since she had got into bed.

A creaking sound had her sitting up, clutching the bedclothes. Someone was wandering around her apartment, turning on lights, running water into the bath!

Pulling open the door, she stared at the shaft of light thrown across the floor, a zipped bag nearby spilling out its contents.

'M-Madoc?' she called softly.

'Who else?' He appeared, towel diagonally across him, drying himself. 'Unless Wilkinson has a key?'

'You haven't got one, so how did you get in?' she answered, ignoring his baiting question and, at the same time, suppressing the surge of longing the sight of his masculinity aroused.

'Left the door on the catch. I went to park my car, get my things.' He fastened the towel around his waist.

'Why—why have you come back?'

He leant against the door frame, arm raised to support himself, eyes sweeping her slight figure. 'I told you earlier why I came. I want you. You didn't think I'd go without getting what I wanted?' His eyebrows quirked, his mouth curved in a faint smile.

'No, you can't. I won't let you.' She turned and ran, slamming her bedroom door and looking around for something to wedge against it. A chair? He'd push that over. She listened, but there was no sound. He hadn't followed.

Breathing deeply, she waited, then called out, 'You can sleep on the couch. There's a blanket in the airing cupboard.' The onslaught she expected did not come and she let out her breath in relief. Maybe his considerate side had taken over, she thought, maybe he was too gentlemanly after all to force himself upon her.

Climbing back into bed, she pulled the cover up to her ears in a childish, defensive gesture. For some while, she lay like that until, of their own accord, her muscles started relaxing and sleep fought a battle for supremacy over her mind.

Sleep won and she drifted off, dreaming that Madoc was making love to her, whispering that he loved no one but her, and that all other women were burnt offerings thrown to him by his family.

'Including Monique?' she murmured in her dream.

'Including Monique,' he answered, then he faded away and she woke up sobbing with happiness. But there were no tears on her cheeks and, worst of all, no Madoc in her arms.

The bed cover was being moved, then someone was beside her, turning her on to her side.

'Madoc?' she asked in a daze.

'Who else?'

'I said you could sleep on the couch! Will you please——?'

'I said I wanted you, and I always get what I want.'

He was unfastening the nightdress, sliding down the ribbon strap. She grabbed his hand with all her strength, endeavouring to still its movement against her breast. 'I thought—I thought you were too much of a gentleman to force yourself on any woman.'

'Oh, I am a gentleman, all through,' was the satirical reply, 'but you're not just any woman.'

His mouth went down and captured a hard pink tip, running his tongue around it until she gasped and clasped his head. 'Madoc, no!' she urged, but found that her hands were holding him to her instead of pushing him away.

He had set light to her passion and she tried to go rigid to stop herself from responding. His head lifted and he reached round to switch on a small, shaded light. 'Come on, my love,' he said huskily, 'remember what we agreed? To enjoy each other without any pretence of loving. Cohabitation without emotion, hm?'

Her words! How she regretted them now. How could she hold back the tide of her feelings, her depth of love for this man, while giving all of herself without crying out her love for him in the course of that giving?

'Touch me,' he coaxed, his voice low, pressing her mouth to his chest. She forgot her promise to herself to hold back and placed tiny, hurried kisses over the rough chest hair, the hard-muscled forearms, the broad shoulders they led up to.

He rolled her against him and she realised he had removed her nightdress when she felt his heated skin setting hers alight. He was hard against her now, and his overwhelming need of her made her arch against him.

He caught her waist between his palms and lifted his head to look her over. He smiled into her eyes, his own turning to a burning amber, like the flare of sunset on the sea.

'You're beautiful,' he murmured. 'Have I told you that before?'

'You have, you have! Madoc . . .' His thighs were pressing on hers, making hers throb. Then he raised her by the hips until she was intimately against him. Her body sensitised almost beyond bearing, she opened out to him.

When he eased into her, she drew a gasping breath. With each rhythmic, possessive movement he was taking her back to paradise, yet she had thought it was lost to her for ever!

Together they reached a pinnacle, staying there, wrapped around in passion, until the golden glow receded. Lynsey opened her eyes and saw the fulfilment and peace in the face of the man she loved.

'Tonight,' he murmured, his face against her breast, drawing breaths and inhaling the scent of her, 'I'll come to you again.'

'I'll be waiting for you, darling,' she promised. 'I'll be waiting.'

CHAPTER EIGHT

She did not hear him go. Waking, her mind still misty with the aftermath of loving, she reached out and found an empty space beside her.

Looking around the flat, she searched for some evidence of his having been there. There was nothing, no stray pen, no discarded tie, not even the sherry glass he had used. He must have washed it and put it away.

Why couldn't he have left some sign of his presence, she fretted, even an indented cushion? Did I dream it? she wondered, but the leap of blood in her veins, her whole pulsating body tone, told her he had indeed been there with her, making love, making her come alive.

Arriving early for work, she made for the telephone on her desk. She would tell him she loved him and wanted to live with him, man and wife, to make a promise that she would never run away from him again.

'Lynsey?' Des Parsons was in the doorway and she let out a cut-off sigh. He eyed her warily. 'How's life?'

'Fine,' she answered happily, and with truth, 'great. Where were you yesterday?'

'On a course at the local Tech. You don't mean you actually came in to *work*? You, wife of the boss, still mixing with the lower orders?'

'No need to be sarcastic, Des.'

'You don't expect me to change my mind about him, do you, just because you've gone and married the guy?'

'What's wrong with him, Des?' she asked gently.

'You're asking me what's wrong with him? Don't you remember the names you called him in the past? He's the enemy, that's who he is. But you're on his side now, aren't you?' he sneered. 'Not so long ago you called him hard and inhuman, didn't you? At his sister's wedding?'

'When I said those things about him, Des, I'd never even met him, had I?'

'If you ever met the man Morgan, you said, you'd tear him into little pieces.'

'I know, Des, but——' She lifted her shoulders.

He wandered away disconsolately.

On the morning after Morwenna's wedding, she remembered, she had told Madoc of the employees' fears about the takeover of Lantern Scientific.

'I suppose you'll be in the front line of the rebellion?' he had joked. *I'll lead it*, she had answered proudly. How naïve I was, she thought, and how careless, considering she had been talking to a man whom she had thought of simply as Morwenna's brother, but who had turned out to be her future employer!

That's all behind me now, she told herself, sorting through the papers on her desk. Those rumours about him were wrong. They must have been about someone else.

Wanting desperately to ring Madoc, to tell him how much she loved him and wanted to make their marriage real again, she darted a glance at Des Parsons. If she used the telephone on her desk, he would listen, she was certain. Downstairs, there was a pay phone in an alcove . . .

The ringing from her desk made her nerves shriek along with the phone bell. Was it Madoc calling to say how happy she'd made him?

'Mrs Morgan?' the brisk voice enquired. Lynsey recognised it. What did it matter, she thought, that he had told his secretary to contact her to save himself time?

'Speaking, Miss Baxter,' Lynsey answered, smiling. 'I was just going to call my husband. Could I just have a word? It'll only take a second.'

'But, Mrs Morgan,' Mary Baxter's voice had a frown in it, 'he's gone away, didn't you know?'

He's what? 'I—Oh, I——' Lynsey moistened her lips, 'I—I forgot.' Away? Why hadn't he said? And what of his promise as she had lain in his arms— 'Tonight, I'll come to you again'? Exactly who had he been talking to—a woman in his dreams? *Monique?*

'Mrs Morgan?' Miss Baxter's voice jogged her back to the present.

'I—er—It was probably a sudden decision?' Lynsey asked, hearing the hope in her own voice.

'Sudden, Mrs Morgan? This trip to China and the Far East was arranged many weeks ago. Mr Morgan is leading a team. It's a very important promotions exercise. They're researching the potential market there ... enormous possibilities. No, it certainly was not a sudden decision.' Mary Baxter seemed extremely put out, as if her integrity had been called into question.

'I—I'm sorry, Miss Baxter, I do remember now ...'

'Mr Morgan left certain instructions, Mrs Morgan. If you are in need of money, arrangements have been made with his bank to let you have whatever you require. His residence in London is yours to use whenever you may need it. He said something else— that his hi-fi is there for you to listen to whenever your sensitive ears—his words, Mrs Morgan—feel the need of it.'

Lynsey went to slam down the receiver, but remembered just in time that the secretary was only carrying out her employer's instructions. 'Thank you, Miss Baxter,' Lynsey said and replaced the receiver shakily.

So Madoc had gone away, and without a word! Last night she thought he had come to her, if not in love, then in affection because he'd wanted her for that special something she possessed for him, something no other woman had given him, when all the time he had been using her—*using her!*—as if she were a . . .

'Lynsey, what's wrong, love?' Carole came to stand beside the desk. 'You're white as a sheet.'

Lynsey could only shake her head.

'David, love, come over a minute. Your sister's not well.'

Lynsey stared up at him. 'I'm fine, honest. I— It's——'

'It's—you-know-who?' David queried. 'What's he after now? I thought it was over between you?'

'It was—it is! But, last night he . . . No, no, I didn't mind, David. I thought it might be a kind of new beginning, but——' she expelled a ragged sigh, 'it meant nothing of the sort.'

'So now what's your opinion of him?' Des Parsons jeered, having overheard. 'Is he back to having horns and a tail in your opinion? Wait till he gets going on us lot. It'll be that——' he sliced his hand across his throat, 'for all of us. You included,' he added as a parting shot.

The late afternoon sun caught at Lynsey's eyes as she stood for a moment on the entrance steps overlooking the car park. Normally, she drank in the gold and the green against the deep blue of the sky, but in that moment, going-home time with an empty evening ahead, the colours of summer almost blinded her.

The hours of that long day had been so shadowed, her vision had grown accustomed to the dull and tarnished look her life seemed suddenly to have taken on. Only now was it dawning on her how much she had lost by running away from Madoc Morgan.

I wouldn't have run, would I, she defended herself, if Monique hadn't stood there in his arms, reaching up for his kiss and telling whoever might be looking—wasn't she an actress by profession?—that the man she was straining against was hers for keeps, no matter how many women he might take on, in succession, in the role of wife.

'Lynsey!' The glass door swung behind her and footsteps caught her up. Sam Wilkinson, taller than she had realised, looked down at her. 'My car's in dock. Could I cadge a lift?' He told her where he lived. 'If it's not taking you out of your way?'

It was, but not badly enough for her to object. Not that she really wanted to. Sam was someone to talk to, to take her mind off the man she really wanted.

Drawing up outside his house, an early thirties construction of solid brick and wide-spanning roof, she rested her arms on the wheel and strained a smile up at him. 'Okay?' she said.

'Thanks a lot, Lynsey.' He made to get out but slowly, stopping partway. 'I'd like to give you a coffee? Or tea, if you'd prefer?' His eyes looked as tense as Lynsey felt. 'The place echoes like a morgue, sometimes, Lynsey, with only me in it.'

How could she refuse? It was a cry from a cracked heart with an off-pitch ring about it. And didn't she know all about cracked hearts? Wasn't her almost breaking?

'Tea would be fine, thanks.' She got out of the car, locking it.

He had been right about the echo, Lynsey thought, stepping on to the woodblocked floor of the entrance hall. In the corner was a small stained-glass window, casting a sombre light across the rug.

A vase of dead flowers stood on a wooden shelf, the decorations needed renewing and there was a heavy, unaired smell telling of days of closed windows while the occupant was out. The touch of a woman was definitely missing.

The kitchen was chaotic, but Sam plunged through to switch on the kettle. He urged her into the living room and cleared a low chair of computer magazines. He nodded to the television screen. 'I spend my evenings with my personal computer playing games against myself.'

This, Lynsey had to remind herself, was one of the two men who, seven years before, had had the initiative to start up a company called Lantern Scientific. It had been successful enough to attract the attention of an international concern like Techno-Global. Where had Sam's initiative gone? Deserted him, it seemed, along with his wife and child.

While he made the tea, Lynsey picked up a newspaper. To her surprise, it bore that day's date. She turned a page and a full-length photograph almost jumped at her. The face, the pose, the poise were all so familiar it was almost as if she were looking at a friend.

Except that this woman was no friend. Monique Merion, the caption ran,

    actress and one-time model, announces the formation of a film company started especially for her. 'My very good friend and top industrialist,

Madoc Morgan,' Miss Merion told us today, 'now turned entrepreneur, has financed this new venture just for me, so I can try my hand at film acting. I shall star in all the films the company makes,' she declared.

When asked what the name of the company would be, Miss Gower replied, Morgan-Merion Productions. And if that isn't enough to set the tongues wagging about Miss Merion's exact place in Mr Morgan's life, then how about this? Wife of four days Lynsey Thorpe, has run out on him, leaving the field—and his bed?—clear for his new business partner.

The newspaper crashed into her lap. Three guesses, she thought ironically, as to who had given them that juicy news item. I don't have to rack my brains, Lynsey thought. But Monique had told the world so much more—how highly Madoc must have rated her abilities to have financed such a venture, and how fond of her he must be to have used his own money to give her her big chance.

'Is that report true?' Sam's hand closed over her shoulder.

'You mean about me leaving Madoc? It's true.'

'So he's the swine we all thought he was?'

Lynsey attempted to fold the paper neatly. 'There were more reasons than one,' she said carefully, 'for my marriage to Madoc. And,' she put the newspaper aside, 'there was likewise more than one reason for my breaking away. Are you going to say you're sorry for him,' she added wearily, 'because your wife deserted you?'

'Judging by that press report,' he handed her a cup of tea, inviting her to sit in an armchair, 'it would seem you were fully justified in your action.'

Lynsey sipped her tea, appreciating its reviving taste. 'I knew about Monique from the start. The trouble is—well, I love him, Sam.' Her voice faltered. 'I still do, but I refuse to share him.'

Sam drew in a sharp breath. 'The man's crazy if he chooses that woman over you.'

Lynsey coloured at the sharp emotion in his eyes and sought a place to put the empty cup in a gesture which indicated her imminent departure. Sam took the cup and moved to sit near her.

He rubbed his palms together and stared at them as if they held the answer to a problem. 'I wouldn't have told you this if you were sublimely happy with Morgan,' he said slowly, 'but since you're not, and have in fact left him, I feel I should tell you, but confidentially, okay?'

Lynsey nodded, settling back again. Her heart jolted as he spoke.

'The research department—he's cutting it.'

Icy fingers walked over her skin. 'Down, Sam?'

'Out. Eliminating it. No reason given.'

'He's told you this?'

'Bill Paine and me, both. Thought we should know because research was our brain child when we started the company.'

The consequences hit her and she went cold. David, Carole, Des—they'd all lose their jobs. And what about me? she thought. Will I get a notice to quit, too? She couldn't see why not, since she had voluntarily ended their marriage, thus putting herself back on the level of ordinary employee.

'Do the others know yet?'

'Official notification's going out as soon as Morgan gets back from his Far East trip.'

'It's confidential, you said, so I can't tell the

others?' Sam shook his head. 'Did you try to persuade him against it, Sam?'

'Bill and I, we both had a go. Like trying to coax an earthquake to change its mind and subside back into the earth.'

Lynsey felt as if she were suffering the aftershocks of that earthquake. 'I must get back, Sam. Thanks for the tea. Want a lift to work in the morning?'

He smiled. 'I didn't like to ask, but——'

'No trouble.'

At the door, he asked, 'Where are you living? Morgan's place in London?'

'Do you know, Sam,' Lynsey frowned, 'I don't even know where that is. I'd feel so stupid asking his secretary.'

'You mean he hasn't told you? Hang on, I'll get the address.'

As she looked at it, Lynsey thought, I bet it's as expensive and exclusive as it sounds.

'Thanks for this. I'm still at my own place. Luckily, I didn't have time to give notice.'

'Seems we're in the same boat, now, Lynsey. Me with my broken marriage, you with yours.'

Was her marriage really broken, she wondered. Shattered to pieces, she answered herself. How could it be otherwise with that report about Monique and the news about the research department?

The former told her Madoc would never relinquish his beautiful actress friend, no matter how many nights he might spend in his wife's bed. The latter told her that his decision to chop research was an act of revenge against her for her desertion of him.

When she and Sam arrived next morning. Morwenna hailed them across the car park. She looked from one to the other. 'You two spent the night together or something?' she joked, but there was a frown behind her eyes.

'Yes, and we enjoyed every minute,' Lynsey joked back. 'Not really, Morwenna. Sam's without his car.'

'You're back at your flat, are you?' Morwenna asked. 'I didn't realise you lived so near to Lynsey, Sam.'

So Morwenna still had her doubts, Lynsey thought tiredly. She had spent most of the night hours wondering how she could possibly save the research department.

'He doesn't,' she said, 'but I didn't mind driving the distance between us to give him a lift.'

Morwenna nodded and went on her way, leaving Lynsey convinced that Morwenna did not believe her.

All day Lynsey longed to tell her brother about Madoc's decision, but she respected Sam's confidence and kept the knowledge to herself.

Once or twice Des eyed her doubtfully. She hoped he would put her withdrawn expression down to the fact that her marriage appeared to have fallen apart before it had even been put together.

During the week that followed, she and Sam often found themselves at the same lunch table. Lynsey was not sure whether Sam had arranged it that way or whether it really was chance.

She did notice that he watched her more, looking at her when she smiled—which was rare these days—addressing her whenever she drifted off, thinking about her own troubled affairs.

'Come for a meal with me tonight?' It was Friday, the end of a week which seemed to have possessed the stretchability of elastic. Sam had issued his invitation across the table and everyone stopped talking to hear her answer.

It annoyed her a little that he had seemed to want the world to know. She was about to refuse when the vision of yet another barren evening flashed across her mind.

'Fine,' she said, aware that David was frowning down at his empty plate.

'I'll call for you,' Sam promised. 'Seven?'

David gave her a questioning glance, and she wanted to shout, 'It's okay, brother dear, when he takes me home afterwards, nothing will happen between us.' Then she thought, if my own brother thinks that's a possibility, what about the others?

Des was wearing a pleased smile, as if he hoped something would happen, if only to make sure that she and 'the enemy' never got together again. Carole just kept on looking at David.

Should I go out with him? she wondered, then remembered that Madoc was subsidising the acting career of the woman who, on his own admission, would always be around for him.

'I'll look forward to it, Sam,' she said, and meant it.

CHAPTER NINE

IT was nearly three weeks since Madoc had left for his Far Eastern tour, but it seemed like three years to Lynsey.

That evening she tried to read, half lying, half sitting in her favourite armchair, but her thoughts kept going back to the evening she had spent with Sam.

At first, he had been charming, making her laugh, but as the meal had progressed, the wine he had drunk, instead of increasing his *bonhomie*, seemed to have made him increasingly introspective.

'I'm useless, aren't I?' he had said. 'My marriage is on the rocks, the firm I helped to start ran out of cash . . .'

'You're fine, Sam.' Lynsey thought it wise to reassure him which, she guessed, was probably what he wanted. 'The man your wife ran to must have been some kind of superman if she preferred him to you.'

She had meant the statement to be a boost to his ego, no more, but he seemed to have taken it as affectionate praise.

'We get along fine, don't we, Lyn?' He had put his hand across the table, inviting her to put hers into it. She knew she would have needed a heart like an icicle to have refused.

After that, he had brightened up and it was not until the evening was nearly over and he was having a final coffee in her favourite armchair that she had realised why. His arms had come round her and his mouth had rooted for hers.

'I like you, Lynsey,' he had murmured, 'you're the sort I should have married, not the glamorous-blonde type my wife is.'

How would it suit me, Lynsey thought, her mind playing with the idea, if I dyed my hair that colour? Would Madoc love me and let Monique go out of his life?

She came back to the present to find that Sam's mouth had not only found hers, but was taking liberties with it which, had she been concentrating on the immediate present, she would never have allowed.

'Sam, no,' she objected, trying to disengage from his arms.

'We're two adult lonely people, so why not? We can comfort each other.'

'It's not comfort I'm after, Sam,' she told him, leaning away from his anticipatory smile, 'it's——' Madoc ... She had so nearly said it! 'Peace of mind,' she added lamely.

'It'll not only give you that, but physical peace, too, sweetheart.' The word held a caressing quality but it grated on Lynsey's nerves.

This, she told herself, was Sam Wilkinson, her ex-boss, on whom she had always looked with respect and admiration. If he'd had a human side—and of course he had—it had never interested her before and it certainly didn't now.

'Sorry, Sam.' She strained away from him and he let her go. 'My heart's a very private thing,' she tried to soften the words with a smile, 'and so is my body.'

He seemed to wince and stood up to go. 'You certainly speak bluntly. I'm not giving up,' he had said at the door. 'One thing I know—you're wasted on Morgan.'

Now, she threw her book aside and stretched at the

window. It was not boredom that was making her restless, it was this hammer-throb of longing that was making her jumpy and tense.

Her transistor radio played her favourite music while she flopped sideways in her chair, her legs crooked over the upholstered arm. For a while, her mind was swept along on the cords and cadences and her muscles gave up the struggle and relaxed.

A crash of discordant sound from the flat beneath hers made her curl her toes and thump the cushion. She wanted to shout, 'Turn your radio down!' but realised that the tenants below might have turned up theirs so as to drown hers.

Switching off the radio, in her mind she heard again Madoc's message via his secretary ... *The hi-fi's yours whenever your ears feel the need.*

Pulling on a long sleeved top over her blouse, she changed her jeans for a skirt. I'll give my ears a treat, she thought, and raced down the stairs.

Half an hour later, she stood outside a row of Regency-style houses ranging along one side of one of London's famous residential squares. The taxi had driven off and left her hesitant, unsure, on the pavement.

The wish—more of a necessity, really, she told herself—to hear good music on the kind of equipment which only a surfeit of money could buy, had carried her along until that moment. Now she was there, she experienced the familiar feeling of wanting to turn and run until life had sorted itself out. The milling, anonymous crowd was a powerful magnet.

Someone pushing against her forced her into positive action. She rang the highly polished brass bell and a voice asked for identification.

'Mrs Morgan, Mrs Lynsey Morgan.'

A male voice demanded, 'Who?'

Having repeated the name—she still didn't feel as though it really belonged to her—the voice said, 'One moment, please.'

So, Lynsey thought, Madoc has a butler. She wondered whether he would be wearing a butler's traditional clothes. A tall, thin man held the door, his carefully blank eyes noting her casual style of dress.

Her surprise clashed with his, since he was as much a puzzle to her as she seemed to be to him. This was no conventional manservant, but a young man dressed almost as informally as herself.

'Mr Morgan's not here,' he said. 'First time you've been here, isn't it?'

Lynsey nodded, stepping inside. Far from annoying her, the young man's manner made her smile. 'I've come in search of my husband's stereo equipment.'

'Oh,' he said, as if that explained everything. 'Along here.' He scooped the air, indicating that she should follow. 'The name's Tom, by the way,' he threw over his shoulder.

The pale walls of the entrance hall, quietly illuminated, rose from soft-pile, brown-speckled carpeting. Doors, heavy and panelled, opened off, while here and there were modern paintings, a chair and a table holding an arrangement of flowers.

A staircase wound upwards and Lynsey experienced the overpowering urge to run to it and sit on a tread to see if a handsome man would climb towards her holding a shoe . . .

She dragged herself back from the past to hear the young man announce, 'This room, madam. There it is. Know how to work the stereo?' She shook her head. 'Okay, I'll show you. What's your kind of music?'

'The classics, Mozart, Beethoven,' Lynsey

answered, then watched while he demonstrated how to work the pieces of equipment. As he turned to go, she said with a smile, 'You're a very unusual butler, Tom.'

He reddened. 'I needed a job. Mr Morgan gave me the chance to learn. I didn't like the idea at first, but it's okay now. I'm a friend of one of his friend's sons. I'm training at a college of catering. Okay? If you want anything, give me a shout. Madam,' he added as if remembering his role.

Solemnly, Lynsey nodded, noticing a bell near the wide fireplace. 'I'll ring, Tom.'

Again he reddened and withdrew backwards.

It was a quiet room, large and, she guessed, probably acoustically excellent. The décor was colour-washed, the lighting half-hidden and subdued. As she pulled the long, apricot velvet curtains, they unfolded themselves elegantly across the windows, their colour matching that of the sofa and chairs.

Across the room stood a grand piano, a Chopin nocturne in place on the music stand, the tapestry-covered stool at the ready. Did Madoc play? Yet another side of him, Lynsey reflected, that I don't know . . .

The melodic tones of Tchaikovsky's Sixth Symphony filled the room as she reclined against the sofa, the beautiful harmonies stroking her thoughts into a tranquillity she had scarcely known since Madoc had entered her life.

Following the classical sound with music in a more modern idiom, she found that it excited her intellectually and, as she listened, she felt her entire metabolism speed up. It was during the slow movement of Rodrigo's Concerto de Aranjuez that the tears sprang to her eyes.

It was all coming back to her—that first moment of

meeting, the 'love' they had made, that wonderful sense of having reached the outermost limits of happiness with the man she had dreamed about all the years before she had even met him, that incomparable happiness which she had been so certain would never fade . . .

Arms gathered her up, lifting her to stand on the floor. A mouth claimed hers and her eyes struggled open, eyelashes heavy with teardrops.

'Madoc?' she whispered, unbelieving. 'Is it really you?'

Am I still daydreaming, she wondered, or did this hard, demanding body of a man have substance and reality?

'Hush,' he said, his lips drinking from hers as if for days he had experienced a thirst that had almost driven him mad. 'Just let me hold you. You're here, in my house and in my arms. That's all that matters . . .'

His hand had found its way beneath her clothes and his touch was exquisite on her breasts, making her senses swim and her body melt against the potent strength of him. It seemed as if he could not get enough of her kisses. Her lips had parted, allowing him entry and her pulses leapt as, slowly, relentlessly, he took control.

The passionate music faded into silence. Reality burst in, cutting down the dreams that hung in the air along with the disembodied notes of music. They stood apart, as if in the presence of a stranger.

At last, he spoke, prising his eyes from hers. 'You came for the stereo sound?' His voice was empty now, devoid of the Welsh lilt she had grown to love.

She nodded. He went across to turn off the cassette recorder, then turned to face her. It's as though, she thought, we haven't even touched, let alone been locked in a passionate embrace.

'You're back early from your trip.' It was all she could think of to say. 'A few weeks, I was told.' Then she remembered that he had not said a word to her about going, even though they had spent the night in each other's arms. All the other accusations with which she had been determined to confront him came piling back into her mind.

'I led the team, got them established and came back. I've just flown in via Hong Kong.' The shadow of a smile accompanied the lift of an eyebrow. 'Any more questions?'

'Yes.' She spoke quickly, before her courage left her.

Slowly, he narrowed the gap, cupping her face and placing kisses all over it. She closed her eyes and clenched her hands to stop them from wrapping themselves around him. The overwhelming need to touch him, she told herself, was purely physical.

'So ask.' His arms were round her again, his teeth teasing her ear lobes, but she tensed against the sensual longing he was bringing to life inside her.

'You're financing a film venture on your mistress's behalf.' She had blurted out the accusation without subtlety or finesse both to harden herself against his caresses and to express the anger and pain which his generosity towards Monique incited.

He did not push her away. Instead, he tightened his grip on her waist and jerked her against his hips, forcing her to feel his deeply aroused state. Only then did he thrust her from him.

His eyes blazed a trail over her breasts and hips and scorched her face.

'Who's been talking?'

'The lady herself, that's who.' She tucked in her blouse and top and ran her hands over her disordered hair where his fingers had pushed into it. 'Telling the world via the media.' She named the newspaper.

'I didn't know your taste in daily papers had sunk to that level.'

'It hasn't. I saw it at——' Her hesitation made him narrow his eyes, but it was too late to stop now. 'At Sam Wilkinson's. I'd given him a lift home.'

'Had you now?' His voice held sarcasm and disbelief. His eyes made an icy inspection of her clothes, making her wish she had taken more care with her appearance.

If only, she thought, I had Monique's style and fashion sense; if only I'd bought that figured silk wrap-around dress I saw in that department store window, and the strappy, pin-heeled shoes that had matched it in colour.

He would have been looking at her very differently now, she was sure; with appreciation and desire instead of derision mixed with contempt.

'So it's Wilkinson, after all?' he rasped. 'At first, I believed you when you denied it. I should have relied more on my own judgment. I've seen you with him enough to have confirmed my suspicions about your relationship with him.'

I could say, she thought wearily, 'There's no relationship, nothing at all,' but he wouldn't believe me.

'You're subsidising your woman friend's career, aren't you?' she accused, then realised that what she had said would sound to Madoc as though she had been trying to justify herself in his eyes.

'I am, yes.' His tone said, it's my business, not yours. He did not say, 'She's not my woman friend.'

His eyes were so cold, she wrapped her arms around her waist. Again she wondered sadly where that warm-eyed, handsome stranger had gone who, a few weeks before, had walked into her life and into her heart.

'Well,' she declared, 'since you think so much of her, no doubt you'll be glad to know she also told the world that our marriage is over. She even hinted that, as your *very good friend*, she was the next in line to share your bed.'

Lynsey had thought he would be angry, but to her chagrin he merely lifted his shoulders. 'Just as you've wasted no time in climbing into Wilkinsons's.'

'You're slandering me, Madoc,' she returned heatedly, 'and Sam, too.'

'Take me to court,' he returned, heavily sarcastic. He looked her over again, his gaze ripping apart her innermost feelings. 'Why aren't you honest, like me? At least I haven't denied that Monique is in line to take your place in my bed.'

So it's true, Lynsey thought with despair. 'She's been there before, many times, hasn't she? I heard that from her own lips that day I left you with her in your house in Wales.'

He rubbed a reflective finger against his cheek. 'You heard it, did you? Which possibly explains your flight from our honeymoon—and our marriage?'

'Yes, it does,' she tossed back defiantly. 'I discovered from what Monique said that the only reason you wouldn't marry her was because her acting schedule wouldn't fit in with your work-load. So you married willing little Lynsey Thorpe who'd cheerfully give up career, freedom of movement, everything, to follow you to the ends of the earth.'

Which was true, she thought with a sigh.

'You know damned well why I married you.'

His cutting tone made her cheeks flare, and all the memories came crowding back, 'I'm sorry,' she said quietly. 'All the same, I wish you hadn't told Monique.'

'Did she put that in her announcement?' he asked angrily.

He hadn't denied, she noticed, that he had told Monique about their reason for marrying, which could only mean that he had.

'Not yet,' she answered bitterly. 'No doubt that's something she intends to do next.'

He looked around. 'Would you like a drink? Didn't you ask Tom for refreshments?'

'Don't blame him, I told him I'd call if I wanted anything. And thank you, but I don't.'

He looked at her for such a long time she grew uncomfortable and went across to inspect the bookshelves set into the wall.

'Did you come by car?'

'Taxi.'

His hands closed around her shoulders. 'I'll take you back to your flat. Unless you intend staying here?'

I'd love to stay here, she thought, trying to take in the book titles. They all appeared to be on the subject of music. 'I wouldn't be welcome, would I?' she asked the books. 'After all, you've probably invited Monique to join you later.'

He swung her round and there was a dark anger in his face. It twisted the line of his mouth. 'Tit for tat, my love? You no doubt have Sam Wilkinson hanging on the other end of the telephone waiting for your nightly invitation.'

Struggling free, she rubbed her bruised arms. 'I'm going,' she exclaimed, cursing her inability to control her trembling lips.

His hand gripped her shoulder. 'This way.'

She had no choice but to go with him. He did not speak a word all the way back. Lynsey congratulated herself on having successfully fought off the tears but, when she spoke, she discovered they were still in her voice.

'Before I go, Madoc,' she asked, her hand on his arm, 'is the rumour I've heard true that you're intending to eliminate the research department?'

He looked at her hand, flicked his glance over her face. She felt it like a whip. He said, speaking every word distinctly, 'I am intending to eliminate the research department.'

A cry escaped her as if a cut had actually been inflicted on her flesh. 'Why, Madoc, why?'

'Make an appointment to see me,' he said savagely, 'and I might tell you.' He leant across, brushing roughly against her breasts. He unfastened the car door, then revved the engine and waited, his hard profile staring ahead.

'Good night, Madoc,' she choked. 'Thank you for the lift.'

The moment she was out of the car, he roared away into the night.

'Still seeing Sam?' David asked next morning, doing his best to sound casual.

'Dating him, you mean? Sometimes. Why do you ask?'

'It's going round that there's something between you. I wouldn't like it if there were, Lyn.'

Lynsey smiled at his concern. 'Okay, I get your brotherly message. It's wrong, in your opinion, for a married woman to have an affair with someone else's husband. Know something, David? I agree with you entirely.'

David smiled, distinctly relieved.

'How could you ever have thought otherwise?' Lynsey chided him. 'We were reared by the same parents, with the same moral guidelines. I've kept to them just as you have. It still doesn't stop me, does it, from having a *friendship* with Sam?'

'Maybe not. But Morwenna's been putting it around that she saw you and Sam arriving together the other morning——'

'Let me get at Morwenna!' Lynsey cried. 'She's my sister-in-law—for the present—and I like her as a person but, like a lot of people, she passes judgment on what she sees, then colours in the rest with her imagination. One thing she hasn't got is the sensitivity of her b——'

Brother, she had been going to say, and looked askance at David.

He had guessed. 'You still love him, Lynsey? So why don't you two get together again? At least, give it a try.'

'He's done it.' Des burst into the large room, his accusation echoing from wall to wall, between the computer equipment, the filing cabinets and office desks.

'Done what?' Lynsey and David swung round.

'Research. It's——' He sliced through the air. 'As from the end of this month. It's official.' He waved a letter. 'There's one for us all, you too, *Mrs Morgan*.' He thrust the envelope at her.

Lynsey took it, her hands shaking. 'There's your answer, David. He's even sacking me, his w-wife.' Her lips trembled and she turned away. It was not the loss of her job that had upset her so much as the way Madoc had done it. To send her a letter, along with the others . . .

Last night, she remembered his callous, parting

shot—'Make an appointment and I'll tell you why.' Recovering, she spun round. 'I'm going to see him.'

'You can't,' exclaimed Carole. 'You're his wife. It'd be crazy——'

'Crazy, Carole,' Lynsey took her up, 'when he actually told me last night to make an appointment to see him if I wanted an explanation of this?' She waved the envelope.

'You don't mean you knew before we did?' Des asked.

'Sam told me, but it was in confidence. I couldn't pass it on under those circumstances, could I? The official notification was going out, he said, when the chairman got back from his travels. Well, he came back yesterday. Hence this. So,' she looked around, 'who's coming with me?'

'All of us,' Des declared.

'He won't see us all,' Carole maintained, watching Lynsey lift the phone.

A few minutes later, Lynsey put it down. If Mary Baxter, Madoc's secretary, had been surprised, she had been professional enough not to show it.

'A delegation of not more than three, this afternoon, three-thirty.'

Des cheered, but no one joined him.

Madoc was ready for them, eyes sharply aware, leaning back, arms folded, against the front of his desk. He motioned them to deep, black leather-covered armchairs, his mouth curved like a jungle animal contemplating prey entirely at its mercy.

He acknowledged each one with a nod. His glance lingered just a little longer on Lynsey, not with friendliness, but in a very male appraisal of the shape beneath the neat blue dress she wore.

'Who's the chief spokesman?' he rapped out.

David and Des looked at Lynsey for guidance.

'I should have known,' Madoc commented dryly. 'As I recall, I had due warning early in our acquaintance.' He looked at her. 'Well, what's your problem?'

'You know what it is,' she snapped. Seeing his raised eyebrows, she amended quickly, 'It's about the disbandment of the research department.'

'You don't like the idea?'

He was playing with them and she wanted to hit out at him.

'No, we don't,' Des replied, 'we'll lose our jobs, won't we?'

'The redundancy payment should see you through until you find another. I'll be generous.'

'It's not just, that Mr Morgan,' David put in, preferring formality even though the man he addressed was his brother-in-law. He was plainly trying to make amends for his companions' lack of tact. 'We feel our section of Lantern Scientific has never been given a real chance. Research of any kind needs money, yet companies hardly ever consider that it's worth more than small fraction of their budget.'

'Research is an important part of industry,' Lynsey put in, looking proudly at her brother and wanting to support him. 'Without it, there wouldn't have been progress in anything, would there?'

'I agree,' said Madoc unexpectedly.

Taking heart, Lynsey demanded, 'So why close us down?'

'Why?' He reached behind him and took up a thick folder. 'I've made a detailed inspection of all research projects currently in hand at Lantern Scientific. The list is impressive but the work done on them is not.'

'It's like Dave told you,' Des said, 'we're short of cash. It's as basic as that.'

David's glance told Des to moderate his tone. 'Underfunded,' David enlarged, 'and therefore very restricted in scope.'

'Underfunded?' Madoc took him up. He flipped through printed sheets. 'Three pieces of new equipment in just over a year. Where are the results? To what use have they been put?'

'We're only a small department, Madoc.' Lynsey used his name spontaneously, but, by his narrowed glance, it was plain that he thought she was trying to soften his attitude. 'If we had more staff, we could give you the results you're looking for.'

'Which brings us back to more cash,' said Des.

'You expect me to throw good money after bad?' he responded sharply, obviously disliking Des's belligerence. 'In my judgment, which, as you have to admit, is what counts, nothing of any practical value has come out of Lantern Research since the day of its inception.' He sliced the folder across the desk behind him. It told of a decision made, one which no amount of persuasion would alter.

David had seen it, too. 'Just give us the chance to prove ourselves,' he pleaded. 'Try giving us more cash and more staff. We're only small—five, plus Lynsey.'

Madoc's arms were folded again, his expression implacable. Lynsey began to despair. The sight of his long, lean body, which she knew by experience to be hard and exciting, made her want to throw herself into his arms yet, at the same time, to batter his chest until he gasped for air. Except that, long before that, he'd have had her own body under tight, relentless control.

'I was right, wasn't I,' she cried, fingertips pressing into the chair's dark, leather arms, 'when I told you before I even knew who you were that the chairman of Techno-Global was callous and uncaring in the way he cut out waste regardless of the human suffering involved? You're proving,' she went on, disregarding the ridging of his jaw and the growing light of anger in his eyes, 'that all those rumours we heard about you were true.'

He moved infinitesimally, as if only by exercising the greatest restraint did he prevent himself from moving across to quell her rebellion physically.

Lynsey knew they had lost the battle—that there had been no real chance of winning it from the start.

'You're inflexible,' she accused, 'you won't even listen to other people's sides of the question. Even a— a computer has more understanding of human needs than you!'

'Lyn,' David pleaded. 'For goodness' sake . . .'

She saw her brother's dismay, stared at her clasped hands and whispered, 'I'm sorry,' then looked to see if her apology had been accepted.

Madoc inclined his head, but his face remained a cold mask.

'Des,' David dipped his head towards the door. He rose, running a finger around the collar of his shirt which, with its tightness from the unaccustomed presence of a tie, seemed to add to his embarrassment.

'Thanks a lot for listening, Mr Morgan.'

'The name, David, is Madoc. We're kinsmen, are we not?' By the coldness in his glance, it seemed that the relationship, via the young woman present, gave him no pleasure.

At the door, David and Des held back for her to pass. She threw one look back at Madoc then went out.

'Lynsey.' His authoritative tone halted her.

David gestured that she must return and whispered that they would wait for her outside. She wanted to say, don't go. The man in the room put such a curious fear into her heart that she felt she needed her brother's support. Yet, he's my husband, she reminded herself, I've lain in his arms, shared the greatest intimacy with him . . .

'Yes?' She had taken two or three steps into the large room.

Her eyes met his to find that his assessing gaze was on her mouth, her breasts, her hips, and her body ached and throbbed as if he were making physical, ardent love to her.

When he found her eyes again, the strong planes of his face became less angled, but his eyes were full of the knowledge of what he was doing to her. His accurate reading of her bodily reactions made her heart pound with mortification mixed with potent longing.

'I can give you a job when the research department goes.'

'When it goes,' he'd said. So all their efforts really had been for nothing!

'Thanks for the offer,' she threw back, eyes blazing, 'but you can keep your sinecure. I can line up at the employment exchange with the best of them, and I do mean the best—David, Carole, Des . . .'

He looked at her steadily, darkly, and she knew she should stop, but the terrible ache inside her still had not been assuaged.

'You accused me once of using my position, and of putting pressure on you to give preferential treatment to one of my relatives. Well,' she raged, 'you can keep your nepotism for one of your own—and I don't mean me!'

She managed to put the door between them, then

leaned against a wall, pressing her fingers into her cheeks. She wouldn't let the tears come—*she wouldn't*. If he came out and saw her, he would know he had won.

CHAPTER TEN

THE telephone rang on her desk next morning. Her heart hit the sky—it could only be Madoc, agreeing to reinstate their department!

'Lynsey?' Her heart nose-dived. 'Sam here.' He spoke briskly. 'Could we meet this evening—a drink somewhere?'

Why not? she thought. I'd only brood all evening, otherwise. 'Why not?' she answered with forced cheerfulness. 'News of your family, Sam?'

'I had a letter from Betsy, my wife. She's agreed to let me see my son, if nothing else.'

'That's great. Tell me about it when we meet.'

'It's not that I wanted to see you about,' he answered. 'Six, after work? I'll take you in my car and we can collect yours later.'

'Fine, Sam,' she answered, frowning.

They were seated in an old world London pub when he told her his reason for wanting to see her. 'Morgan's fired me,' he said, staring into his half-empty tankard.

Lynsey sat completely still, holding her breath. Then she let it out, lips parted. It couldn't be true. 'You're fooling, Sam, you must be!'

'As from tomorrow. I've cleared out my desk, put all my belongings in the car.'

'But, for heaven's sake, on what grounds?' she asked.

'Incompetence. That just about sums it up. Can you imagine how I felt?' He turned heavy eyes towards her. 'As if I haven't got enough on my plate.' He picked up his beer, started to drink it, put it down. 'I said things to him I shouldn't have—he got me so mad.'

'What kind of things?'

'Like—well, when you were free and I was free, I wanted to marry you.' As she gasped, he said, 'I wanted to hurt him, Lynsey, pierce his armour, get under his skin.' He shook his head and took a mouthful of drink. 'For all the effect it had on him, I might have been telling him the state of the weather outside.' He shook his head. 'He's a swine, Lynsey, all we heard about him was true. He's using a guillotine on personnel, not just a scythe! Heads are rolling with a vengeance.'

He covered his eyes, clasping his other hand into a fist on the seat arm.

'I'll——' She had to take a drink to moisten her throat. 'I'll see what I can do. Except—well, I'm not exactly his favourite person today. Yesterday he gave the chop to research. I knew about it through you, but the others were devastated. In the afternoon, we confronted him. No, he confronted us. It was like meeting a leopard in the jungle.'

Sam looked sympathetic.

'All the same,' Lysney promised, 'I'll have to do something. It tears me to pieces to think of you out of work, along with all the other difficulties you're facing.'

He took her hand and played with it. 'Don't get yourself into trouble with him over me.' He looked at her. 'I meant what I said. I'd like to marry you when we're both free of our present ties.'

Lynsey shook her head. In the circumstances, she could not tell him, after Madoc, I don't want any other man. I wish I'd given our marriage more of a chance. I threw something away that might have been good one day ... But would it—ever? With a relationship based only on sexual compatibility, and with another woman constantly on the sidelines, how could it have succeeded?

'I still can't believe it, Sam.' She listened to the voices around them, raised in laughter or in friendly argument. 'What about Mr Paine?'

'Bill? He's fireproof, older than I am, more experienced. According to Morgan, he's got all the virtues I lack.'

Lynsey pushed back her chair. The unfairness of Madoc's action had come full at her. A picture had flashed across her mind of Sam sitting at home, lonely and without hope, family or job. If it was at all within her power, she would at least get that job back for him.

Tom, the trainee, butler said, 'Who is it?'

'Mrs Morgan, Mrs Lynsey Morgan.'

'Okay, one sec—one moment, please.' Lynsey smiled in spite of herself. There was a pause and she started to fret. 'Still there—er, madam? Mr Morgan says you can come in, but you've got to cut it short. He's got a date.' A brief pause. 'Er—he's otherwise engaged this evening.'

The door was opened and Tom, looking smarter than before, grinned at her. 'Follow me. This way.'

Madoc, wearing evening clothes, stood beside a low, marble-topped table, staring down at various items spread over it. He seemed to have to tear his eyes away from them.

So, Lynsey thought, he's putting me in my place. The room did little to boost her confidence. Its spacious elegance both dazzled and dwarfed her.

Here the paintings were classical and gracious. They were, she guessed, not reproductions. The décor was a delicate green, all the furnishings having been chosen to match or to tone. This London residence, far more than his house in Wales, revealed the extent of his wealth.

As Madoc raised his eyes, hers dropped to look at whatever had engrossed him so deeply. They were portraits of Monique, large professional photographs, some in black and white, others in colour. The poses ranged from the falsely coy to the overtly sensual.

The surge of jealousy she experienced nudged against the anger that had brought her there and they were an explosive force. His eyes held no welcome, nor did he invite her to sit down.

'You wanted to see me?' he asked, icily polite.

She knew exactly how Sam must have felt on being confronted by this pitiless man. She too wanted to get under his armour and dent his supreme self-assurance.

'You've sacked Sam Wilkinson. He's just told me.'

'So now you know.'

'How could you, Madoc! He's one of the founders of Lantern Scientific. What have you got against him that you could take over the company he helped to establish, then throw him out? He and Bill Paine——'

'Are two different people. If that's all you've got to say, you can get out of this house.'

Lynsey backed away, horrified by his attitude. 'Madoc, we're still married . . .'

'We are? That's news. I heard from Wilkinson's own mouth that you and he plan to marry the moment he's free of his wife and you from me.'

'I know he said that, but it's not true and he didn't mean it. He told me he said a lot of things he didn't mean. He just wanted to annoy you.'

'He thought telling me he planned to marry my *ex-wife* would *annoy* me?'

His biting sarcasm appalled her. 'You're victimising him,' she hit back. 'Just because he and I have had a few drinks together——'

'Is that all you've done together?' he said nastily. 'I had it from him that he'd held you in his arms, kissed you, taken you to bed. Deny that if you can.'

'I do deny it——' she hesitated, 'the last part, anyway.'

'So you admit you and he have made love?'

'Kissing and hugging, no more, I swear.'

'Isn't that enough?' He was advancing towards her. 'Maybe the bedding of you is on the agenda. Think of the opportunities you'll both have to get together when you're both out of work.' He seized her arms, jerking her back and forwards. 'No doubt you're delighted now that you turned down my offer of a job when your present one disappears. It leaves you free to be his constant companion.'

'So you admit your sacking of him was purely vindictive?'

'I admit nothing of the sort.' He released her and pocketed his hands.

Lynsey smoothed her hair, waiting a few moments to get her breath back after his manhandling of her.

She met his eyes and he looked so handsome, she felt her heart would break. Handsome for his date—who was his date?

'I dismissed him for pragmatic, not emotional reasons. From the start, he's been obstructive, uncooperative, argumentative. He questioned every move the board of Techno-Global made where Lantern are concerned. He also betrayed something told him in the strictest confidence—that of the closure of Lantern's research. Not exactly a glowing testimonial.'

'He can't have been all those things,' she protested. 'He's reasonable and open to suggestion. He and Bill Paine have been two of the best employers anyone could wish for.' Madoc was plainly unconvinced. 'You can't have handled him properly,' she finished, her voice rising in her effort to persuade him.

Three steps brought him against her. 'You're very strident in his defence,' he snarled, gripping the front of her brightly patterned shirt. 'I think it's time, don't you, that I handled you *properly*.'

He twisted her sideways, his hold tightening the neck of her blouse and making her gasp. He caught the gasp with his opened lips and proceeded to draw the very breath from her body. His arms moved to encircle her, holding her down and probing the innermost recesses of her mouth and forcing her to cling to his shoulders.

When her eyelids fluttered closed and her body grew compliant under the force of his kiss, he raised her and tugged open the blouse buttons, lifting her breasts free of her clothes and transferring his mouth to them.

She writhed under the coaxing movement of his lips, her nipples hard under the rough caress of his tongue. His hands found the bareness of her waist, massaging it, slipping round to explore her firm, tautened stomach.

He was making her ache for him, the blood in her body leap and burn with longing for him and the assuagement of her clamourous desire.

'Madoc, Madoc,' she choked, 'you must stop . . .'

'Why?' he derided. 'So as to leave you untouched and eager for Wilkinson's attentions the moment you go back and report the result of your advocacy on his behalf? Not on your life!'

He tugged the blouse from her shoulders and went for the side zipper on her skirt. She resisted with all her strength, but it made no impression. He was wild with an angry passion and she did not possess the strength to repel him.

In the distance, the door bell pealed. He paused momentarily to listen and she managed to twist from his hold and retrieve her blouse, pulling it on, her eyes still fighting him.

'Your date,' she said hoarsely, her mouth dry from his plundering. 'You'll be able to satisfy your carnal appetite now without a struggle, won't you?' Her fingers were unsteady as she fastened the buttons, yet he watched her antics with a cool amusement that maddened her.

'Yes, I will,' he answered equably, smoothing his hair but otherwise betraying no other sign of disarray.

Tom's knuckles on the door demanded attention. 'Your date's arrived, Mr Morgan. Er—Miss Merion to see you, sir.' He peered in and barely suppressed a grin, having plainly sensed the tumultuous atmosphere. Then he stood back and, with a flourish and a mischievous smile, motioned the new arrival in.

'Darling?' said Monique, looking from Lynsey to Madoc. 'You're expecting me?'

There was a touching quaver in her voice and an appealing uncertainty about her movements that would have melted the hardest masculine heart. It seemed to have turned Madoc's to water. He extended his arm and she needed no further invitation to move across and snuggle into the circle of it.

Lynsey lifted her head high. 'Goodbye, Madoc,' she said. Outwardly, she had regained her composure but her thoughts and emotions felt as if they had been battered to the ground by a whirlwind.

If she had hoped he would answer, *au revoir*, she was disappointed.

'*Da boch*, Lynsey,' he replied, 'which, in Welsh, means goodbye.' There was no mistaking the finality of his tone.

'Come for a chat,' Morwenna invited. 'Bring a friend.'

'If Sam comes with me,' Lynsey answered, eyeing her sister-in-law warily, 'will you start another rumour that he and I are sleeping together?'

Morwenna coloured just a little. 'Well, couldn't I be forgiven for putting one and one together——'

'And making three?' Lynsey broke in. 'No, you couldn't. Did you really think I'd start an affair with another man so soon after my own wedding—and so blatantly, too?'

'Well, you did leave Madoc. That was a bit of a scandal in itself, wasn't it? You should have heard my mother going on to Madoc about how he should have married Monique after all.'

'And what did he say?'

'That it was his life and if he made mistakes, he would answer for them.'

So I'm one of his 'mistakes', am I, Lynsey thought, sick at heart. Her temper started to rise at Morwenna's attitude. 'Are you going to keep on being rude to me,' she retorted, 'or do you really want me to accept your invitation?'

'These things have to be said,' Morwenna replied, 'and it's always better to get things off your chest where relatives are concerned.'

'Relatives, maybe,' Lynsey conceded, 'but you could

lose friends that way, you know. And we are friends, aren't we, as well as being related through marriage?'

'We are. Okay, so you're bringing Sam. No rumours, I promise.'

Griffith, round-faced, toughly built, welcomed them, a drink in his hand. 'What will you have now?' he asked, his Welsh accent strong.

'Sherry, please,' Lynsey told him, going to the window.

The setting sun had turned the cooler air golden. She stared out at the garden where, on the evening of the barbecue, Madoc had rescued her from the garden flare. In the summer-house over there he had asked her to marry her.

The memories she had of their past relationship, she mused, turning back to the room, were salted like tears, and bitter to the taste.

'A beer for you, Sam?' asked Morwenna, patting the sofa cushion beside her.

Lynsey sat there, while Sam lowered his slightly stooping length into a chair.

'Morwenna, I like your outfit,' Lynsey exclaimed.

'Pure woollen tweed from Wales,' Morwenna supplied, rubbing her fingertips over the fabric of the skirt and matching waistcoat, the delicate grey and lavender pattern distinctively Welsh.

'I saw signposts to craft shops and woollen mills,' Lysney reminisced, 'when Madoc took me around on our honeymoon. I wanted to visit them, but——'

'If you'd let your honeymoon run the full four days,' Morwenna remarked bluntly but drily, her expression bearing an uncanny resemblance to her brother's, 'he would probably have been delighted to take you round them.'

Griffith held up his glass. 'Cheers, *lechyd da!* as we Welsh say.'

'I doubt if Sam feels like cheering,' said Morwenna. 'I was sorry to hear, Sam, you've felt the iron hand of my dear brother. Or should I have said sharp teeth?'

'He can certainly bite,' Sam commented with irony, 'and wield a flashing blade when cutting his opponents down to size.'

'And out of their job,' added Griffith, with a rueful expression. 'It's glad I am that my brother-in-law is not the head of the company I work for. He'd have me and my colleagues by the scruffs of our necks. He'd say we enjoyed our jobs too much, we look so happy. We spend a lot of the day talking, but we work hard, too.'

Morwenna stretched out a fond hand and squeezed his arm. 'It's a terrible reputation my brother has. He's got high standards and expects everyone else to live up to them.'

'Except himself, you mean?' Lynsey said. 'If they were as high as you imply, Morwenna, he would have put Monique out of his life the day I married him, wouldn't he?'

Morwenna sighed and lifted her drink to study it. 'Don't ask me what part she plays in his life now. I thought you might be able to tell me, Lynsey. I do know,' Morwenna went on, 'that he's sunk a lot of money into the film company he's formed for her benefit. If that's anything to go by——'

Lynsey took a drink of sherry too quickly and choked. So even Madoc's sister suspected that Monique was his mistress.

Sam patted her back and let his hand remain until Morwenna's eyes swung round to him questioningly. He leaned back and swallowed from his glass.

'How do you like your new leisure?' Morwenna asked him.

Sam shrugged. 'Not much. It gives me too much time to think.' He drank again. 'I hate to see what he's doing to Lantern Scientific.'

'He believes that pruning gives a better tree when it finally blooms,' Morwenna replied.

'The secateurs he uses hurt the branches he prunes,' said Lynsey, making a face. 'Research is a marked department.'

Griffith laughed. 'Marked *down*, you mean, don't you?'

'Well, you're free of his terrible influence for a week or so,' Morwenna told them. 'Madoc's gone to America—with Monique.'

Three weeks later, a memo arrived on the desk of every employee of Lantern Scientific.

'It's ironic, isn't it,' said Carole, waving hers, 'that it comes in our last week here?'

'Bet he timed it that way.' Des made a tearing motion with his piece of paper. 'If I don't attend the annual get-together of Techno-Global, he can't sack me, can he? I've already been fired.'

'Haven't we all,' David said, reading his memo again. 'It's at his house in Wales. Near Llanwrst, it says. Isn't that where you spent your honeymoon, Lyn?'

That was the part that had upset her—Madoc had invited her, formally, along with the others, back to the house where, for so short a time, she—and she had thought he—had experienced a taste of paradise.

'Will you go?' Carole asked.

Lynsey nodded. 'It'll be the last time I'll see the place, won't it?'

Carole, detecting an unintentional note of sadness, shot her a look of sympathy.

'*If* I go,' Des stated, 'it'll only to be eat and drink at the boss's expense. He owes me, and I'll squeeze every cent out of him I can, even if I have to get stoned out of my mind to do it.'

The others laughed, but Des frowned and walked heavily away.

The few days to the weekend passed quickly. Lynsey worked hard finalising the notes that David and the others had made, even though it was their last week in the job.

On Friday evening, they went to a local pub for drinks and a farewell meal. Lynsey's heart wasn't in it, and the others tried to cheer her up. She thought, with irony, that it was the reverse of what had happened at Morwenna's wedding.

It was she who, then, had attempted to brighten their mood as they had discussed the consequences of the coming takeover. She had run up those stairs, hadn't she, and lost her shoe. It might, she thought, have been interesting to speculate whether she would have met Madoc Morgan had she stayed in her seat and been miserable with the rest of them.

To everyone's surprise, David offered to pay for the meal. Carole asked if he'd been left money by a rich relative and, if so, shouldn't they get married before he squandered it all? He laughed and reached cheerfully into his pocket, even buying them all a final round.

At first light next morning, they set off in David's car for north Wales, Carole beside her fiancé, Lynsey and Des in the rear seats. The other members of the research team had declined the invitation.

Aunt Dilys, round-faced and welcoming, held out

her arms. Lynsey stepped into them, needing the comfort and the reassurance at such a time.

'What a foolish man my nephew is to let you go,' Dilys soothed, her words muffled by Lynsey's cloud of hair. 'And so happy you looked the day of your wedding, when you stepped through that door.'

Lynsey straightened and smiled at her.

'I shouldn't have left you now, should I?' Dilys teased, her smile sorrowful. 'I wouldn't have let you escape the way Gwyneth and Dan did.'

Lynsey went to the window of the small guest bedroom to which Aunt Dilys had shown her.

'It angers me so, my dear, to have to bring you here. My foolish nephew phoned me from Los Angeles especially to tell me to give you a room here and not to let you book in to hotel accommodation with the others. But not into his room, he said. You—his wife, too!' She had left, shaking her head.

Where was Madoc now? Lynsey wondered. Was he coming back for the annual celebration? She knew in her heart that there was no need for the chairman of any giant company to attend such events, especially, she thought acidly, when his woman friend was already tagging along, available whenever he wanted her.

Shafts of late summer sunshine sparkled on the swimming pool. The hills and distant mountains were as remote as Madoc had become, their slopes and summits as formidable as his eyes and manner the last time she had seen him. 'Goodbye,' he'd said and, from their total lack of communication since, he had plainly meant it.

When Madoc had shown her round—how long ago that seemed now!—she had caught a glimpse of the room she was now in. Then, she had thought it charming and had pictured her parents staying with them and sleeping in that bed.

It had never for a second occurred to her that she would ever occupy the room herself—as a guest in her husband's house. Sighing, she started to unpack, shaking out the dress she had brought to wear that evening.

It was the dress she had worn when she had first met Madoc, the one he had told her he liked so much. Had she been nostalgic, she wondered, hanging it in the wardrobe, or foolishly hopeful in bringing it?

The latter, she decided—she was there as an employee of Techno-Global, no more, no less, like David and Carole and all the others. Her status as the chairman's wife counted for nothing now, even if she was staying the night in his house.

If he did bother to attend, he wouldn't be alone, would he? The woman he really loved would be by his side.

By now, he would have accepted Monique's offer to give up her career and go with him everywhere. Hadn't she demonstrated how truly she had meant the statement, by accompanying him on his present trip to the United States?

Lynsey shared the lunch table with Aunt Dilys. David and the others had booked in, at the company's expense, at a small, family guest-house nearby.

When Dilys discovered that Lynsey's brother was one of the guests, she called the others on the phone and invited them to spend the afternoon hours at Madoc's house.

Des wandered round, a little dazed, watching the preparations for the buffet meal and ostentatiously licking his lips as bottles of alcohol appeared, crates full of them, one after the other. David and his fiancée walked in the gardens, while Lynsey talked to Madoc's aunt.

'He's a philanthropist, is my nephew,' Dilys commented, taking time off to snatch a cup of tea.

'Madoc—a *philanthropist*?' Lynsey exclaimed. 'But that's a person who does good to others! He has a terrible reputation, Aunt Dilys, for sacking employees he considers redundant, regardless of how they and their families suffer. Over-manning, they call it in the business world.'

Dilys nodded. 'Businesslike—now that's something he certainly is, dear, and should be, shouldn't he, a man in his position? But ruthless? Well, Morwenna should know her own brother, I suppose.'

She drank some tea and reminded Lynsey to drink hers.

'Let me try and explain what I mean,' Dilys went on. 'Dan, now, Gwyneth's young man—he was out of work and Madoc gave him a job.'

Lynsey nodded, saying thoughtfully, 'There's Tom, too, who works for Madoc at his London house—Madoc offered him a job, too, if he agreed to train for it.'

'See what I mean, dear?' Dilys asked, easing herself out of the chair. 'No, you stay a while. I'll see what those caterers are up to.'

So Madoc was generous and altruistic, was he? Lynsey thought angrily. Even when he closed down an entire department, regardless of how many he put out of a job?

'Mrs Morgan!' Gwyneth almost bumped into Lynsey as she made for the stairs. 'Nice it is to see you again. Is Mr Morgan with you? He's still missing, see.' She looked furtively from side to side. 'I got into terrible trouble, didn't I, for letting you go that day.

And my Dan, too, for driving you to the station to catch the train. He was in a stew, was Mr Morgan. I can't remember seeing him so angry.'

'With you or with me, Gwyneth?'

'The three of us, Mrs Morgan. I nearly lost my job, you know.' She smiled broadly. 'You won't ever ask me to help you run away again, will you now?' She lifted her hand and hurried on her way.

Cars were swinging into the drive and filling all the spare corners. Lynsey leaned out of the guest room window and strained to see if she could recognise Madoc's car, but there was no sign of it. She began to wonder, also, if Morwenna was coming.

Sighing, she combed her hair until it fluffed and swirled above her shoulders. Renewing her make-up, she fixed pendant gold earrings into place and pushed a matching bracelet on to her arm—the only two items of jewellery Madoc had given her. He hadn't had time to give her many things, had he? she asked, smiling wryly at the joke against herself.

The evening was a glowing red-gold, the far mountains becoming even more mysterious as a gold-tinted autumnal mist laid a veil across them. The pool was a shimmering blood red now, and someone had switched on the underwater lights.

All this, she thought, gazing through the window that overlooked the cultivated garden, while the wilder parts stretched into the distance—all this beauty and this splendour could have been mine if I'd opted for the 'submissive wife' role; if I'd been prepared to play second best to Monique's prime place in Madoc's life.

She told herself—a conclusion finally arrived at—that she had done the right thing in leaving him. She had kept her self-respect, even if she had lost the man she loved. But, she thought, he was never really mine to lose, was he?

The door burst open and Carole threw herself in, uncharacteristically boisterous, dressed attractively in a slim-fitting dark dress that flattered her well-shaped figure.

'Come on down,' Carole urged. 'The party's begun. And, would you believe it, Sam's arrived.'

Lynsey swung from the window. 'Sam was invited? He never told me.'

'Seems he couldn't make up his mind. But since it was all expenses paid, he came. He's looking for you.'

At least I'll have a partner, she thought, nearing the stairs with Carole beside her.

'Des has found a girl,' Carole said, 'a fair-haired type from one of Techno-Global's subsidiaries. She's gazing up at him adoringly. You should see the pair of them!'

Carole hurtled down the stairs but Lynsey lingered, leaning over the banisters and watching the mêlée below. Older people stood together, drinks to their mouths, eyes watchful and waiting.

Younger people, having pepped up their metabolisms and freed their inhibitions with pre-party drinks were, like Carole, in high spirits. A group of them dashed in and out of rooms, generally making free with the chairman's house; whereas she, Lynsey, on seeing it for the first time as the chairman's bride, had trod with awe and admiration around its elegance and luxury.

Aunt Dilys stood on the sidelines, watching benignly. She, Lynsey guessed, had seen it all before, and—she thought with a smile—together with the house, had lived to tell the tale.

The moment Lynsey saw Sam, he looked up and

saw her. He lifted his glass and smiled winningly. She started down, but froze on the third step.

There was a commotion at the main entrance door leading in from the drive. Everyone went quiet, people seemed to be holding their breaths.

Madoc Morgan stood in the doorway, a beautiful, dark-haired woman at his side. Her slender body was wrapped in leopard-skin print, her arm had slipped through Madoc's. Her whole demeanour shouted to everyone present, *This man is mine!*

Madoc saw the girl at the top of the stairs. There was no warmth in his eyes, no pleasure at seeing her again.

'Hi, Madoc,' said David, near the front of the crowd, lifting his hand with a surprising familiarity.

Still Madoc stared at Lynsey and a re-run of their first meeting flashed across her eyes. But this was not the man who, then, had come to her as if hypnotised, holding her shoe like Prince Charming to her Cinderella. This was a stranger who seemed about to order her off his premises.

Slowly and with all the dignity she could muster, she finished the descent and went across to Sam's side. It looked like a woman going to her lover. In reality, she felt like a child running for protection to its father's side.

Madoc gave a slicing, dismissive look and escorted Monique into the one room which had been designated 'private'. The noise level rose, the party had begun.

'Lynsey, hi!'

'Morwenna,' Lynsey exclaimed, 'I began to wonder if you were coming.' How happy she looks, Lynsey thought, not just happy—radiant. A powerful feeling, very much like envy, threatened to overwhelm her.

Her marriage is working, she thought, why didn't mine? But what a world of difference there was between Griffith, Morwenna's husband, and Madoc Morgan ... The one like an affectionate spaniel, the other with the fangs of a tiger.

'Griff had an important meeting this morning.'

'On a Saturday?'

Morwenna laughed. 'It proved, he said, that he and his fellow workers do actually work, even if it's only outside working hours! Hi, Sam.' She grinned up at him. 'You look smart. Got a lady friend to look after you?' Her eyes rebounded off Lynsey and back to him.

'No, Morwenna,' he said, unruffled by her baiting, 'I thought it wise to keep up appearances when coming as a guest to my ex-employer's house.'

She laughed again. 'There'll be dancing soon. Madoc usually leads, with his chosen partner.' She frowned, looking doubtfully at Lynsey as they both remembered Monique. It was plain that Morwenna was thinking, it should be you. 'See you later, Lynsey,' she said. 'We'll have a "young wives" meeting, shall we?' She swung away, waving cheerfully.

Lynsey wondered what she meant by that, but nodded all the same. A drinks salver moved past and Sam grabbed a glass for Lynsey.

'They said he had a good side,' Sam commented enigmatically. 'Seems it might be true.'

Lynsey licked the sherry from her lips. 'Who?'

'Morgan. This morning I received a cheque through the post. It's why I came.' He took a drink while Lynsey stared. 'Redundancy payment, the letter called it. Didn't know I was entitled to any, the way he fired me. Even if I was, I didn't think he'd pay.'

'Was it—a lot, Sam?'

He told her the amount, and she gasped. 'Philanthropic', his aunt had called him. Was it true, after all?

'Enough to enable me to sell my place and get a better house. I'll be able to ask my wife to come back to me, to try and mend our marriage.'

'That's great, Sam.' Lynsey's eyes shone.

'It was one of her grumbles—that I wouldn't move to a better area when our circumstances improved. When I do——' his eyes softened with emotion, 'we'll be a family again, my wife, young Terry and me.'

Touched to her depths, Lynsey squeezed his arm, her smile full of encouragement. 'She'll come back to you, Sam, I'm certain she will. Here's to you both.'

She drank the toast and Sam joined her, putting his hand over hers on his arm. 'You've been my support all this while. I don't know how to thank you.'

Lynsey turned her head as if someone had tugged a string. Across the room the chairman of the company was staring at them. She snatched her hand away, angry with herself for feeling guilty over an action that had been motivated solely by sympathy.

It had looked as though Madoc was about to approach her. Soft strains of music drifted over the lively, excited crowd. Madoc turned away and lifted his arm in a gesture of invitation.

Monique emerged from the 'private' room, hair immaculate, figure swathed from shoulder to ankle in a golden dress. She looked breathtakingly beautiful. Even Sam was entranced.

Joining her body to Madoc's, she leaned against his arm and followed wherever he led. They made a perfect couple and the audience—wasn't Monique, Lynsey thought bitterly, playing the role of her life?—could only stare in wonder.

So now I know, Lynsey thought—Monique is Madoc's 'chosen partner'. But had she ever really doubted it?

Lynsey stayed with Sam, dancing with him now and then, lining up together at the tables groaning under the weight of food. Occasionally, she caught glimpses of Madoc moving from group to group, and always Monique was beside him.

Aunt Dilys mixed and wandered, waving to Lynsey, clearly loving every minute, every person there.

Sam went off to fill their glasses and Carole spotted her standing alone. She raised her arm in a waving salute and Lynsey returned the greeting, spying her brother's laughing face. She wondered at his high spirits and decided that it hadn't registered on him yet that, from Monday on, he and Carole would have no job. Near them stood Des, gazing at his pocket-sized blonde-haired partner.

'Lynsey.' The deep voice brought her round and she stared into the twin icebergs of her husband's eyes. He looked her over and she knew that he had recognised the dress. 'You look well.'

'Thank you,' she answered tautly, her heart twisting at the sight of the familiar features, their strength of character, the firm, angled facial structure, the fine, full lips. It was as though he was mesmerising her, using some inward force to draw her closer, bringing her mouth into contact with his. With all her will-power, she resisted the pull, asking calmly, 'Did you enjoy your stay in America?'

Here we are, she thought, talking as politely as strangers, yet we've been lovers, knowing each other as intimately as two people can.

'It was a business trip, no more, no less. As such, I didn't find it particularly enjoyable.'

'But Monique was with you.' She took a breath and it resisted release. Would the innuendo anger him?

'Monique was with me,' he answered evenly. 'From that point of view it went excellently.'

I bet it did, Lynsey thought, imagining Monique's arms winding round him in the night. Her jealousy must have shown since Madoc smiled. It was not a tender smile, nor even a pleasant one. It mocked and tormented and scorched her heart.

The moment Monique reached his side, sliding her arm round his waist, Sam closed in against Lynsey.

'Good evening, Mr Morgan,' he said with extreme politeness.

Madoc nodded. 'Wilkinson.'

Sam made a great play of handing Lynsey her refilled glass.

'It's what you like, isn't it, Lyn?' he asked with a purposeful tenderness. 'I think I know your tastes by now.'

Madoc's eyes swung from one to the other and Lynsey felt her face sting as if he had hit her.

'Darling,' Monique purred, 'you know my tastes in everything by now, don't you? But everything,' she whispered, straining her mouth towards his, only to remove it sulkily when he did not respond. 'I want to dance, darling,' she added, winsome now, like a little girl.

With a terrible shock, Lynsey saw that she wore an engagement ring.

Sam put his glass aside and took Lynsey's from her. 'Dance, Lyn,' he invited and swung her on to the floor.

She did not resist. Her mind was asking over and over, How could he—*how could he*—let her become engaged to him while he's still married to me?

'Why?' she asked Sam, meaning, why the show of affection, as if we were lovers?

'You ask me that,' Sam answered, 'when that sultry bitch was hanging on your husband's every word? Sex was in her eyes and bed—his bed—was in her thoughts. I knew exactly how you felt. My marriage has broken up, too, hasn't it?'

Has my marriage broken up? Lynsey wondered, answering herself severely, you know it has. How can you doubt it now she's engaged to him—even if it is at present a token engagement? Accept the break-up, put it behind you. If only I could, she thought, if only I could stop loving that man ... *I shall have to, won't I, now she's his wife-to-be?*

CHAPTER ELEVEN

'LYNSEY.' A loud whisper came from behind her. Morwenna was beckoning. Sam had drifted a few paces to converse with an old friend. Morwenna joined her.

'Our "young wives" talk, remember?' Morwenna said, tugging at Lynsey's arm until they were across the hall and in a quiet corner. 'I've been wanting to tell you all evening. It's just been confirmed—we're expecting, Griff and me.' Lynsey looked blank. 'A baby, silly, a bonny bouncing baby. Seven months from now, I'll be a proud mum. Oh, Lynsey,' she hugged her, 'we're so pleased. Griff can't wait to change its nappy, he said!'

'Morwenna,' Lynsey tried to untwist her heart-strings and give a semblance of a smile, 'wonderful news. I'm delighted!' And I am, she thought, I really am. 'Mind which?' she asked. 'Which variety, I mean?'

Morwenna shook her head vigorously. 'It can be twins, or triplets,' she exclaimed. 'They'll all be welcome, all the same or a mixture!' She careered away, waving. 'See you around—had to tell you ... You're the first to know, after the parents and Madoc.'

A chord of music, louder than the rest, slowed the dancers to a halt. The chatter and laughter fell away, leaving only the subdued clink of glasses.

It was obvious to everyone that there was to be an announcement. Madoc lounged to one side, arms folded, jacket removed, tie loosened, a faint smile underlining thoughtful, watching eyes.

Was it coming, Lynsey wondered, hands curled stiffly, lungs almost forgetting their function, the announcement that would link Madoc's future with Monique's?

David, having miraculously acquired a tie, stepped up on to the rostrum. He sought for his sister among the crowd, then spoke.

'The boss,' he glanced over his shoulder at Madoc's seemingly indolent figure, 'the boss has told me to get up here and tell you something. It affects some of the people here, but its waves will be felt eventually throughout the whole structure of Techno-Global.'

Was the announcement, Lynsey began to wonder, not the one she feared?

'Some of us,' David was saying, 'have been done away with.' A roar of laughter greeted his words. David grinned. 'I mean, of course, made redundant. Des here, and Carole, my fiancée, not to mention my sister over there. There are a few others, too, who aren't present.'

The tension in Lynsey's muscles started infinitesimally to relax its grip. The guests waited, their laughter lingering in their eyes.

'Well,' and it was as though David was producing a trump card, 'as from next month, we won't be out of work any more.'

Lynsey's heart began to race.

'The board of Techno-Global,' David announced, 'has made the decision to form an off-shoot—a new company, in fact.'

There was a deep silence as he consulted his notes, then read from them. 'It's going to be devoted entirely to research, not just attached to Lantern Scientific, but Techno-Global as a whole.'

Lynsey's heartbeat started hammering and she

looked Madoc's way, trying to signal 'Thank you'. He raised his eyebrows as if to say, Now call me uncaring and inhuman if you dare.

'It's got a name already,' David was saying. 'It's going to be called——' he consulted his notes again, 'Foresite Limited—with us into the future. Okay?' He thought for a moment, then added, 'It really should be Foresite *Unlimited*, shouldn't it?'

There was another burst of laughter.

He looked round again, catching Madoc's approving nod. 'Thanks for listening,' he added and joined his friends.

There was prolonged applause, then chatter and back-slapping, as if the guests themselves had achieved a goal.

Des gave a shout and stared about for Lynsey, raising his hands in a boxer's triumphant salute, then swung his new girlfriend around by the waist.

Lynsey pushed towards her friends, meeting Aunt Dilys. 'I told you, dear, didn't I,' she commented happily, 'Madoc's a real philanthropist. I hope you believe me now.'

David and Carole untangled themselves and David's arms hugged his sister. 'Thanks a lot, Lyn,' he muttered. 'Okay, I know you're going to say you had nothing to do with it, but——'

Her eyes shone at his pleasure. 'Don't thank me, David. The chairman,' she declared with a mischievous smile, 'doesn't believe in nepotism. He told me. I tried him out, you see, and——'

'So it was the super talent of Lantern Scientific's research staff that did it, after all,' he teased.

'When did Madoc tell you?'

'Ten days ago. He met a group of us. We had some long talks.'

'Ten days? But he was in America then.'

'He came back for a few days especially to discuss his plans.'

'So you knew in advance, yet you didn't tell?'

'Strictest confidence,' David answered immediately. What he didn't add was, and we all know what happens to people who betray Madoc Morgan's confidence, don't we? His glance had sought out Sam.

'No wonder you've been so free with your money lately,' Lynsey joked. 'And full of the joys of living, too.'

'Life's great at the moment, Lynsey, just great.'

I'm glad, she thought, really glad—for David, for Carole, and Des and Morwenna . . .

A baby, Morwenna was going to have a baby . . . The music had started again, louder now, as if the players had been infected with everyone else's happiness. Lynsey, standing alone, put her hands to her ears. Dancers swirled around her. She was imprisoned by swaying, vivacious bodies. She had to get out, get free . . .

The music followed her stumbling steps, almost deafening her. She found herself in the hall, but people were there, too, eating and drinking. She elbowed her way to the kitchen, bursting in.

'Mrs Morgan,' Gwyneth exclaimed, 'whatever's the matter?'

Lynsey shook her head, making for the exit.

'You're not running off again, are you? I'll be sacked on the spot if I let you . . .' Gwyneth's voice followed her into the chill night air, the slam of the door cutting it off.

Lynsey fled across the cultivated gardens, making for the outlying trees, but she didn't reach the woodland. The lighting did not go beyond the flowers and the shrubs, so she followed the double row of coloured lights strung along the path leading to the pool.

At its edge, she halted, watching with wild eyes the gilded, moving water slapping against the tiled sides. A shadowy reflection of herself was there, floating on the surface, like a drowned person drifting aimlessly ... As I shall be, she thought, after Madoc and I have finally parted.

And now Morwenna was going to have a baby—the words echoed over and over in her head. It would be the child of the man she loved. With all her heart and soul, Lynsey longed to be like Morwenna, telling the world her joyful news, telling Madoc—*telling Madoc*.

She saw a poolside chalet and ran towards it, trying the door. A hand gripped her outstretched arm and she gave a cut-off scream.

'Come here,' a man growled and she was swung round roughly against his chest.

'No, I won't!' she shrieked, tugging away.

'You're here and you'll stay,' he rasped, holding her against him.

The feel and male scent of that hard, lean body was so familiar her head spun and she closed her eyes. 'I'm expecting a baby,' Morwenna's lips mouthed against the blackness, 'a baby, a baby ...'

A long, painful sob shook her slender frame. 'I want your baby,' she heard herself whisper, her face muffled by the hard chest. 'Your baby,' she repeated, rolling her forehead against him. The tears dampened the shirt fabric, smooth to her skin. 'At least give me that before you leave me for Monique.'

He seemed to have acquired the substance of a carved, stone figure.

'I won't trouble you after that, Madoc, truly. You'll be free to go on your way, taking Monique with you.'

He had started breathing again, but there was no comfort in him for her, no warmth, no tender touch.

'All I ask,' she sobbed, 'is the loan of a room in your house until the baby's born——'

Without relaxing his hold, he selected a key from his pocket and unlocked the chalet door, pushing her in front of him. The glow from the pool's underwater lighting filtered through the windows, sliding over his features in a pale and dark pattern. The lines and ridges of his face were cruel in the eerie light and his expression held no mercy.

'You've got it all worked out, haven't you,' he said through his teeth. 'You'll be telling me next that you'll have the baby all on your own, then you'll get out of my life and you'll never see me again. Women do that sort of thing to a man these days, don't they?'

He seized her arms, holding her away, his fingers bruising, his face white and rigid. 'I'll never see the child, will I, I'll have no access to it, no loving contact, no rights as a father. So,' he released her and her arms ached with the sudden cessation of his merciless pressure, 'I'll give you no child. You understand?'

She could only stare at him, holding her face, her hands trembling. 'No,' she choked, 'I don't understand, not now that I'm your wife.'

'My wife,' he snarled, 'you have the audacity to call yourself my *wife*?' He stared contemptuously. 'There's a willing male not far from here. He'll grant your request with alacrity, judging by the way he looks at you and won't leave you alone, not to mention the wide-eyed way you've been gazing at him the whole evening.'

Her clasped hands just wouldn't stop shaking. 'How can you make such accusations about my relationship with Sam Wilkinson when you take Monique with you wherever you go? You talk to her as if she were the most precious thing in the world. She looks at you as if she worships you. You can't deny it!'

He looked at her coldly, making no attempt to answer her challenge.

'All I've done with Sam is share meals with him, go out with him sometimes, and listen to his domestic troubles. Whereas you—you've never given Monique up. Everywhere you go, she's there, too. You've financed a film company for her sake. You've just come back from a trip to America, taking her with you.'

'I took her with me,' he answered tonelessly. 'As I told you, it was a business trip. Its aim was to promote the film she's currently making with that film company I backed—for business reasons,' his smile was a taunt, 'a purely pragmatic venture with nothing emotional about it.' The words to Lynsey sounded familiar.

'Likewise, she came with me—for business reasons. Now do you understand?'

Lynsey shook her head.

'Never mind,' he murmured, eyes busy outlining the shape of her, and smiling with a kind of brittle pleasure at the feverish light in her eyes. 'It will keep.'

He moved towards her, the outside illumination adding menace to his face.

As he advanced, curled fingers unfastened his shirt buttons, revealing the broad expanse of chest and dark mat of hair and Lynsey longed to rub her cheek against them, listen to his heartbeats and inhale the individual scent of him.

'Come to me, Lynsey.'

She backed away. 'Why? What are you going to do?'

'Oblige a lady. You see, I've changed my mind. You

made a request, a very special request. It's not every day a man is asked to father a child.'

Step by tantalising step, he followed her backward retreat to the door, reaching past her and turning the key.

'No, no, Madoc,' she whispered. 'I've changed my mind, too. All right, it—it might be possible to cohabit without feeling or affection as we agreed on our honeymoon, but to me it's wrong for two people to conceive a baby without loving each other. You love Monique, not me. She'll have your child.'

He caught her arms and jerked her against him. 'Oh no,' he growled, his hands in a brutal hold on her flesh, 'you will be the one who bears my child, you and only you.' His eyes had darkened, his jaw thrusting forward with an age-old lust. His fingers found the zipper on her dress, sliding it slowly down her back.

'You think I'd let you go now?' His hand was drawing the dress from her shoulders, his heated breath tingling sensuously on her smooth, white skin. 'Let you go to Wilkinson and make your *special request* to him? If procreation's the name of this game, then the child brought into being under the cloak of our marriage will be mine and mine alone!'

The dress shimmered to her feet and he lifted her free of it even as her body struggled to stop him. 'No, no, Madoc,' she protested wildly, 'I want any child I have to be conceived in love. Do you hear me?'

Her words hung on the air unheeded. With a hard, sensual gaze he stroked the whiteness of her body as it glowed in the subdued light.

'I've dreamed of this,' he muttered, lifting away the lacy cups that covered her breasts, and substituting his hand, stroking, moulding the piquant shapes and bringing them to a straining fullness in his palm. 'I've dreamed of making love to a woman with your irresistible beauty, one who moreover begs me to take her, who pleads with me to give her a child—one of mine, no less, no other man's but mine.'

His head lowered and his mouth played with her softly swelling breasts, his tongue drawing circles around the hardened rosy tips. Lynsey's head went back, her breaths coming quickly, the pleasure he was giving her making her urge her body towards him. Her hand smoothed the back of his head in small feverish movements.

Why, she asked herself, why am I letting him do this to me when I know he's not experiencing even a spark of tenderness, let alone affection? Because I want his child, that's why, because I was so unhappy when it didn't happen the last time. *Which is why I didn't tell him on the morning of the wedding.* I wanted another chance to have his child!

He was crouching on his haunches now, closing his hands around her hips, her stomach hardening and quivering under the stimulation of his stroking thumbs, the whisper of his kisses across its highly sensitised surface. As her skin grew cool under the touch of the chill evening air, it penetrated the shining haze encircling her mind that he had removed the rest of her clothing.

He must have noticed the faint tremor of her flesh beneath his touch, since he straightened, all the while divesting himself of his own covering. Then he stood before her as naked as she and she was mesmerised by his firm, strong body, loving every lean and muscled line of it.

'Cold?' His eyes skimmed her face, his hard stare sliding over her figure. He lifted her arms wide, gripping her wrists and she felt defenceless under his slow and intimate examination. 'I shall warm your lovely body under mine, *fy nghariad*, my love, when I've fed my desires to their limits with the sight of you.'

Small darts of excitement made her flesh tingle at the undisguised male hunger in his stare. When he dropped her arms and cupped her face, pulling her mouth towards him, the pulsing heat of her loins flared into a burning need as they made searing contact with the aroused and powerful desire in his.

His mouth took hers in his control, intruding and searching out its secret depths. Holding the kiss, he eased her backwards, forcing her to her knees. She braced herself for the impact of the wooden floor but found the softness of an air bed waiting to receive her.

He knelt in front of her, stroking her forward until their bodies made explosive contact. Still he did not break the kiss, but leaned back and took her with him, all the time caressing her flesh and invading her most secret places.

He eased her sideways and down and then he was over her, still kissing her with an intense and demanding thoroughness that had her moaning at the ecstasy of his mastery and giving little throaty, pleading sounds as she came more and more under his spell.

At last he moved his mouth from hers, but at once her lips strained forward towards his as if the kiss had been like nectar and she could not live another second without its heady taste.

But he held away, laughing as her mouth rooted vainly for his. Panting, she urged him, 'Now, oh please, Madoc, I want you, I need you, this minute.'

Still he did not take her. He took his time, a hard

smile playing over his mouth as if he enjoyed tormenting her. His lips skimmed to her throat, his hands stroking and playing, and wherever they went his lips followed. He lifted her hips and his mouth roamed intimately until she gasped and twisted in her ecstasy.

He raised his head and his eyes blazed into hers, their needs and their desires merging into a locked and burning gaze.

'Now,' he told her, 'now I'll take you, when *I* am ready ...' Only then did he allow her to feel the demanding pressure of his complete arousal and her thighs opened to him, her overwhelming love for him exulting in the thrust and drugging rhythm of his complete possession.

'I love you, Madoc!' She heard her own voice cry out the words, and then repeat them time and again. The fierceness of their coming together did not die away and she clung to him, raining tiny kisses over his mouth and shoulders and chest.

A smile crept into his face while his eyes stayed shut, and he pulled her even closer, holding her still. She was quiet then and a lovely languor overtook her, making her tunnel into him and lie replete while the storm of loving slowly died away.

It was a long time before he moved from her but even when he did, he still did not release her. 'I want you close,' he said softly. 'I want the mother of my child-to-be so near it won't be possible to get even a breath between us.'

His body held hers in an encompassing embrace, his legs entwining with hers, the upper part of her body engulfed in his arms. 'If you went away,' he muttered, as if to himself, 'it would kill me.'

Those words, how clearly she remembered them. He had murmured them that first time he had come to her room. Then, she had thought they had been meant for someone else, for another woman in his life. Now she knew they had been meant for her—hadn't they?

Lynsey stirred and turned into Madoc's arms—except that she must have awoken from a dream since there were no arms to hold her. Madoc had gone.

Listening to the silence, she grew fearful. Was Madoc so regretting what had happened between them he couldn't wait to get away?

Opening her eyes and sitting up, she saw that he had at least cared enough about her to have covered her with his jacket. A light was on—a desk lamp on a table across the large room. The chalet looked as though it doubled as Madoc's hideaway whenever he wanted to shrug the world off his shoulders.

Scrambling up, she wrapped the jacket around her and went to the window. Stars were high in the sky and the moon sailed across the cloudless, dark expanse. A lone, shirt-sleeved figure was at the pool's side, hands in pockets, staring at the water.

Lynsey tapped on the window and Madoc's head turned. She gave a small tentative wave thinking he would come in to her but he nodded without moving. Disappointed, she glanced around, seeing a door which was half opened.

There was a shower cubicle in the tiny bathroom and this she stepped into gladly, noticing water droplets on the tiled wall which revealed that Madoc had recently been there.

Dressing hurriedly, she gazed in the wall mirror. Her make-up had gone, but no water on earth would be able to wash away the brilliant colour in her face, the dancing delight in her eyes. Happiness, she decided, was the best make-up in the world.

'Madoc?' She hurried outside, pushing her arm through his and straining to look into his face. His profile, stern and chilling, was all she could see. Her delight started on a downward path and she wondered if it would ever find its way up again.

'So what's your plan now?' His question came impassively out of the darkness and her heart fell low, low into the lapping water at their feet. 'To return to Wilkinson until time reveals whether our activities tonight were successful?'

It can't be true, she thought, after all that's happened between us, he can't still be thinking this way!

Lynsey withdrew her arm. 'You're—you're talking as if you were just a—a——'

'Stud?' He looked at her at last, but with irony. 'Isn't that all you want? My child, you said. The delivery date on an order like that can't always be guaranteed.'

Misery gripped her stomach and she felt physical pain. Nothing had changed between them, had it? What did I really expect, she wondered bitterly, a grand reconciliation scene, paradise regained? He doesn't love you, he loves Monique, she admonished herself, can't you get that into your stupid head?

Insects darted over the water's surface, attracted by the undulating reflection of gilded light. Behind them, party sounds hung on the air. Techno-Global's annual festivities were still in full swing.

'I don't have any plans,' she replied. 'Where Sam's concerned, I can only say again that all I've been doing is giving him moral support in his efforts to get his family back. Believe that or not, Madoc, it's the truth.'

'Why aren't you honest and admit he's your lover?' Madoc thrust at her. 'When I asked if Wilkinson's allegations about the lovemaking between you were true, you didn't deny it.'

'There wasn't any lovemaking! We—we kissed once or twice——'

'Which meant nothing, of course.'

'Of course it meant nothing.' His sarcasm infuriated her and she accused, 'What about you and Monique? I've watched how she wraps herself around you every time you're together. I haven't noticed you pushing her away.'

'She's an actress, therefore she acts, no matter what the occasion.'

'I'm sorry, but I can't believe you.' It gave her little pleasure to throw his sentiments back at him. 'You see, on the night of the barbecue, you told me something I've never been able to forget. Whether you married me or not, you said, Monique would always be around.'

'So? It was true then,' he admitted carelessly. 'It's true now. She's around.' He saw Lynsey's puzzled stare. 'She still exists, she lives and breathes.'

Lynsey hardly dared to breathe. 'Is that what you meant by that statement? Truly?'

'Truly.'

It was like a glimpse of blue in a black, storm-filled sky, but Lynsey dared not admit its existence. If she reached out to touch it, it would surely slip away.

'But you're engaged to her,' she said sadly.

His head came round. 'That's news to me.'

'I saw her hand. She's wearing an engagement ring.'

'Of course she is, it means precisely what it's telling the world—that she's an engaged woman.'

'Who—who to then?' Slowly, slowly Lynsey's heart

lifted from the depths. Was the moon really shining just a little more brightly, or had its silvery glow invaded her eyes?

'Remember those portraits of her I was looking at the day you called on me?'

'The black-and-white photographs?'

'Publicity shots. The man behind the camera is the man Monique has decided she loves better than any other man in the world, even,' he added drily, 'me.'

'That photographer's her fiancé?'

'He's her fiancé.'

There was a splash and Lynsey saw the spreading, golden circle the pebble had made as Madoc had tossed it in.

'Oh, Madoc,' she heard herself reprimand, her happiness racing up the hill down which it had so recently fallen, 'you shouldn't ever throw stones into a swimming pool. No pool owner in his right mind——'

He turned and caught her by the hips, his eyes gleaming in the reflected light. 'Who said I'm in my right mind?' His tone matched the gold fleck in his eyes. 'Do you really expect me to stand aside and let the woman I love run back to the lover who's waiting for her?'

'Madoc, oh Madoc, you said——'

'I said—it's a pity to spoil this lovely dress, *fy nghariad*.' His voice was full of laughter and intent and, suddenly, they were falling sideways.

Locked together they hit the water, going under only seconds after Lynsey had gulped a mouthful of air. When they surfaced, Madoc was still holding her, hair flat to his head, shirt billowing out, eyes brighter than the myriad of stars above them.

'Madoc,' Lynsey gasped, feeling her dress clinging to every curve of her tingling body, 'did you hear what you said?'

'That I love this woman in my arms? Is it not the truth you want to hear, *fy nghariad*? *Rwyn dy garu di*, I love you, Cinderella, have loved you from the moment I set eyes on you as you scampered up those stairs and challenged every man within hearing to be your Prince Charming.'

'But Madoc——' She shivered in spite of trying to suppress it.

'Hush,' he said, 'this conversation is best carried on on dry land. Don't you agree?' He stroked her wet hair, pulled her the length of him and kissed her until little throaty sounds came from her throat and she was gasping for mercy. Then he propelled her towards the pool steps and swept her, dripping, into his arms.

'But, darling Madoc,' Lynsey probed much later, when they were dried and dressed in towelling robes they had found in a cupboard, 'that night you made love to me and you proposed, I didn't think you meant it.' They were sharing a garden chair, Lynsey on Madoc's lap, her arms around his neck. 'I thought you only said it as a way of reassuring me, a woman you fancied for the night, that I meant just that bit more to you than——'

'No man,' he said sternly, 'goes around proposing marriage to one-night stands. Especially when the girl he takes to bed with him has everything he has been looking for since he became aware of the differences between the sexes—everything you possess, my love, in your mind and body.'

He placed soft, breathing kisses around her throat. 'Didn't I whisper in my sister's ear after I'd met you at her wedding that I'd just found a needle in a haystack and that she had dark brown hair and eyes to match and a shape that had been made for my arms to fit around? And didn't she ask who it was, and I said she'd know soon enough?'

'You said all that to her, so soon after we'd met?'

'I meant every word I said, both to her and to you, every promise I made, *cariad*.'

'Even,' she whispered in his ear, 'when you said it would kill you to——'

'See you go? Every syllable and every word of it.' His brown eyes glinted. 'But you did go.'

'I'm sorry, I'm sorry.' She buried her face in his neck and his arms tightened around her. 'I'll never listen to rumour again. The people who knew you best gave me a very different view of your character.'

'And rumour was wrong?'

'Completely wrong.' She slipped her hand inside his towelling robe and rubbed her fingertips over his chest. 'I haven't said thank you yet, for that new research company you've formed. You've made David and Carole and all the others so happy.'

'Glad you're pleased about that, but,' he slipped his hand inside her towelling robe, making her squirm as he found the hardening, rosy points, 'there was nothing emotional about it, it was purely a pragmatic decision.'

She smiled at the familiar phrase. 'One more thing, darling.' She gripped his wrist, stilling it so that she could concentrate. 'That day I left you—on our honeymoon—I heard you tell Monique the real reason why you married me.'

He frowned, shaking his head. 'You're mistaken.'

'But I did. You said, "I married her because——"' Try as she might, Lynsey could not recall the exact words. Her eyes opened wide. She had not heard them. Her imagination had filled in the rest of the sentence. 'What did you tell her, Madoc?'

'That I'd married you because I loved you.'

'Oh, Madoc,' Lynsey exclaimed, 'if only I'd known, I wouldn't have left you.'

As his mouth came down, her arms reached up and wound around him. 'I'll never go away again. You see,' she murmured, 'like you, I've found everything I've been looking for—in you,' she whispered, snuggling even closer.

And it's true, she thought mistily, parting her lips to his. Here in his arms, knowing he loved her every bit as much as she loved him, she had found that elusive paradise at last.

Coming Next Month

Available in February wherever paperback books are sold, or through
Harlequin Reader Service:

In the U.S.
P.O. Box 1397
Buffalo, N.Y.
14240-1397

In Canada
P.O. Box 603
Fort Erie, Ontario
L2A 5X3

Six exciting series for you every month... from Harlequin

Harlequin Romance·
The series that started it all

Tender, captivating and heartwarming...
love stories that sweep you off to faraway places
and delight you with the magic of love.

◆

Harlequin Presents·
Powerful contemporary love stories...as individual as the women who read them

The No. 1 romance series...
exciting love stories for you, the woman of today...
a rare blend of passion and dramatic realism.

◆

Harlequin Superromance®
It's more than romance... it's Harlequin Superromance

A sophisticated, contemporary romance-fiction
series, providing you with a longer,
more involving read...a richer mix of complex plots,
realism and adventure.

Harlequin
American Romance
Harlequin celebrates the American woman...

...by offering you romance stories written about American women, by American women for American women. This series offers you contemporary romances uniquely North American in flavor and appeal.

◆

Harlequin Temptation
Passionate stories for today's woman

An exciting series of sensual, mature stories of love...dilemmas, choices, resolutions... all contemporary issues dealt with in a true-to-life fashion by some of your favorite authors.

◆

Harlequin Intrigue
Because romance can be quite an adventure

Harlequin Intrigue, an innovative series that blends the romance you expect... with the unexpected. Each story has an added element of intrigue that provides a new twist to the Harlequin tradition of romance excellence.

Harlequin Books

PROD-A-2

HARLEQUIN HISTORICAL

Explore love with Harlequin in the Middle Ages, the Renaissance, in the Regency, the Victorian and other eras.

Relive within these books the endless ages of romance, set against authentic historical backgrounds. Two new historical love stories published each month.

HIST-B-1